MICHAEL REALIZED THAT HE *COULD* HAVE EVERYTHING —YOUTH, SUCCESS, MONEY, PARIS. AND LISA. AND HER LOVE. OR WAS HE JUST DREAMING?

We put our arms around each other. Real tight. I could feel Lisa's body and it was firm, and well, giving, against mine. There seemed to be only us. And the sky. And Paris. I'm not sure a kiss would have meant what holding her meant. Not just then, anyway. Besides, it was so typical. *Something* would keep us apart . . .

ABOUT THE AUTHOR

MURRAY KALIS (pronounced KAY-liss) has written for television and motion pictures. Film production has taken him on location in the Far East, Morocco, England, Scotland and France—especially Paris, where he is a frequent visitor. In the United States, Mr. Kalis divides his travel time between New York and California. When not in motion, he is currently at work on a new novel.

LOVE IN PARIS

by

Murray Kalis

FAWCETT GOLD MEDAL • NEW YORK

LOVE IN PARIS

Published by Fawcett Gold Medal Books, a unit of CBS Publications, the Consumer Publishing Division of CBS Inc.

ISBN: 0-449-14382-1

Printed in the United States of America

First Fawcett Gold Medal printing: January 1981

10 9 8 7 6 5 4 3 2 1

À Daina

Nous serons ensemble encore.

Chapter

1

WAS it the time in my life for her? Or was it being in Paris? Whichever, she was innocent. About life. About the world. And yet in other ways she was the oldest twenty-two-year-old I'd ever met. In a restaurant on the Rue de Chabrol, I made a toast to her beauty. "Say 'To our love,'" she corrected me. "With love you will always see beauty." Anyway, that's what I think of. The romance. Her and Paris. It's nothing like the films I'm in. After all, you can't plan how love will go. It just happens.

It was my last night in Paris and I hadn't seen anything outside our locations. The filming had taken up the entire two weeks, and frankly I was a little pissed about it. They had talked of returning to do some interior shots, but that was still a maybe. So I decided just to cut out on my own and get some kind of feel for the place. I mean, Paris is *the* city and it wasn't so far into September that it was too cold to walk

7

around. Besides, I had been trying to make the trip since I graduated from college, some seven (God, is it that many?) years ago.

Of course, I wasn't really getting off on the idea of dining solo. But no way was I eating with the crew or cast for the ten millionth time. Nor was I looking to getting fixed up with some movie "hopeful."

I decided to try to get lucky.

Standing and waiting for a streetlight to change, I got into a quick conversation about things to do with a couple of girls from Brazil, now living in Paris. Both married, so no help there. Fortunately, their English was good enough to give me the name of a restaurant their French friends said had a great bouillabaisse: La Méditerranée.

My next attempt was in a sidewalk cafe on the Rue de l'Opéra. Thanks to my French not being any better than the girl's English, there was some general confusion over whether she accepted my invitation to dinner. She must not have because she didn't come along when I left.

From there I bought a map of the Métro system (why cab it when I'm trying to get into the place?) and set out for La Méditerranée. This meant getting off the subway at the Odéon stop on the Left Bank. When I came up it was raining. Terrific. My plan was to take a walk around the block and say "Hi" a lot. I figured these were students, and I represented a free meal. How could I miss? I'll tell you how. True, there were lots of gals, but they were all answering in French, which did me no good at all.

Back at the Métro entrance, I decided to work the other side of the street before giving up. I crossed in the rain and started walking. Looked like a total bustout night. Maybe it isn't so neat to be where nobody knows who I am. I started looking for a taxi back to the hotel.

As I passed by a café there was a girl inside whose green-blue eyes followed mine for just a little longer than an instant. Was this the look? My cynical side said she was probably daydreaming—my guardian angel told me it couldn't hurt to check her out. So I walked back in front of the café. Really, what else does a twenty-eight-year-old actor and (I hoped) rising star have to do besides walk up and down the Boulevard St. Germain in the rain? She didn't even give me a glance this pass. Well, it wasn't like I had anything else going. I shuffled into the café and sat down two tables away, so as not to be obvious.

This done, I could get a better look at her. Her hair was kind of light brown going to gold at the tips, which touched her shoulders. I decided her face was definitely within acceptable limits. Her nose was almost straight with just a hint of a bump at the bridge to keep it from being boring. Maybe the mouth was a tad small, but the lips were full with a hint of a kind of knowing smile. She was dressed like a student (which figured for the area) but not grungy or unkempt. Just a white turtleneck and jeans. I was waiting for the right moment to say *"Parlez-vous anglais?"* when the waiter brought her a plate of fries and a Coke. He said a few words to her in French. French? Oh-oh, not looking good for the home team, fans. He walked over to me. I decided to order *en français*.

"Ca-fay o-lay see-voo-play."

There. Not only would she think I was a man of the world, but I wouldn't spoil my dinner. She stopped the waiter when he passed her table.

"Pouvez-vous m'apporter la bouteille de ketchup, s'il vous plaît?" she asked.

Hold it. Hold everything. What was with this ketchup jazz? And in that tone of voice? "Catch-up." I was being had. All my hesitation left me, and I turned to her.

"Hey, I'm trying to find a restaurant," I intoned in my broadest American phrasing.

She studied me with those green eyes flecked with blue which brought me in there in the first place. I decided I had better keep rolling.

"It's called La Méditerranée," I went on, taking out my guidebook. "It's supposed to be very good."

"I've heard of it," she said, without any French accent whatsoever. "I think it's supposed to be very expensive."

There is a God. Now if I can just hold on. I got up and sat down next to her. "Here's the address," I said, showing her the page.

"That's about three blocks from here," she said.

She pronounced about *a-boat*. Maine, perhaps? We'll get into that later.

"How'd you like to have dinner there with me?"

She motioned to her Coke and fries.

"I just got dinner."

I figure when all else fails you can always fall back on honesty.

"Listen, this is my last night in Paris and it'd be a real drag to eat by myself," I pleaded. "I'll pay for your fries."

Would that do it?

"Okay on dinner," she said, pulling on a heavy knit blue cardigan, "but I'll pay for the fries myself."

If you think the rest would be easy, let me correct that impression. Lisa insisted on walking—she wouldn't let me pay for a cab, either—and she had absolutely no idea where we were going. She wanted to prove she knew her way around Paris, or at least the Left Bank, and I believed her for about the first half-hour. Let's face it, I'm not a big fan of walking anyway, especially on an empty stomach. That, the misty rain, and the pace she set with her long-legged stride (not that she was all that tall compared to me, especially given I am a trim five eleven and one-half) made me start waving for a cab. However, I wouldn't say the walk was a complete waste. I found out she had come to Paris to study French politics three months ago, took some heavy political science courses at the Sorbonne, added French lit and art history to that, and, most important, wasn't dating anybody regularly.

The taxi took us back to a couple of blocks away from where we started. Fortunately, La Méditerranée justified the buildup. I was sure I saw Shirley MacLaine there (I had seen her once in Hollywood) and pointed her out to impress my date. It wasn't necessary; the restaurant was more than enough. She may have even realized she was underdressed.

"Some place," she said as the maître d' took us to a table for two by the window. "Where we met is my idea of a big night out."

I ordered for us both: escargots, the recommended bouillabaisse, and salads. The white wine I handled nicely by asking for it by number (no sense in risking mispronunciation). I also ordered a bottle of Evian water, which irritated the wine steward. The hell with him, I was thirsty.

I decided to move things alone.

"Now that we're sharing snails together, can I ask you something personal?"

"Give 'em a snail and they want to move in." She smiled.

"What's your name?"

She laughed at the oversight.

"Lisa Foster," she said.

"I'm Michael Shymkus," I said, waiting to see if she might recognize it.

"Shymkus?" she repeated. "Isn't that Lithuanian?"

Okay, she didn't recognize the name. Well, for a change it was nice to be with a girl who wasn't in the biz.

"My father's father was from Lithuania. The rest is kind of mixed."

The wine steward brought the wine and let me try it. Pouilly-Fuissé. It really was excellent. I wondered why she wasn't more curious about me.

"Well, it's sure nice to do some work in Paris." As soon as I said that, I hated myself.

She nodded and the golden ends of her hair bounced above her shoulders. Yeah, nice. Real nice.

"It's nice to be in Paris for any reason," Lisa said.

"Not that I won't mind going on to Scotland," I said, trying to keep the conversation going—at least until I could tell her what I did. "It's supposed to be beautiful."

"I've never been there," she said.

They brought the bouillabaisse. I decided it was so good, no matter what happened the evening wouldn't be a total write-off. I think Lisa felt the same.

"Michael, this is delicious."

"At least it takes my mind off the movie I'm making."

What was that? Worse than the "working" statement. A total non sequitur. Would she respond?

"You're a director?"

Goddamn! The *auteur* theory again. What about performance? Interpretation?

"I'm an actor," I corrected.

I couldn't tell exactly how impressed she was. Obviously she hadn't heard of Michael Shymkus, even though *New West* magazine mentioned my name kindly in reviewing my supporting roles in two earlier features. Actually, it was the reviews and my television work which brought me to the attention of the executive producer of this picture. That, and my pain-in-the-ass agent who gets me to the right parties with the right people, and insists that every moment of my life be devoted to my Career.

"Oh," she said.

"I'm playing the lead in this film," I said.

"Oh, again," she said.

A French song was playing. A very pretty tune. We watched the raindrops making trails on the window. Was there so little to say? Could I have intimidated her by saying I was in the movies? More like it, she didn't care. She was a student, right? Probably only saw foreign films. I had to laugh; for all my trouble, this was going nowhere fast.

"How did you know I wasn't French?" she asked.

Since there was no one else at the table, I figured Lisa must be speaking to me. I responded with rapt attention.

"Huh?"

"You just started speaking to me in English, remember?"

"It was the ketchup," I said.

"The ketchup?"

Now I'll teach her for putting on airs with me.

"You really had me going," I allowed, "but when you said you wanted ketchup on your fries I said to myself, 'this chick's gotta be American.' "

She smiled, as if she realized she was about to regain something of her mystery.

"Ah, Mr. Hollywood, but I'm not an American. I'm Canadian."

I came back quick, with no mercy.

"Oh, I did hear an accent," I pointed out, "when you said about—I mean, *a-boat*."

"And you don't have an aaak-cent?" she countered, referring to the last vestige of my Chicago birthplace.

This had gone far enough.

"Tell me, Lisa, now that you know I'm just another bourgeois American over here to make money, would you still give me a look like you did at the café?"

She didn't skip a beat.

"Sure, you're sexy."

Something told me I was in a lot of trouble.

The important thing is to go for it. I have learned through extreme remorse that I am sorrier for the things I haven't done than the things I have.

Of course, Lisa's last statement really threw me. Something a little more shy and uncertain would have suited me better. My taking the aggressive macho part and all that, you know?

It was still raining lightly as we walked back to the Boulevard St. Germain. I decided to make my big play.

"You want to come to my hotel for a drink?" I offered.

"No, I would like to, Michael, but I can't. I really have to get home. I've got an early-morning meeting on the Paris city elections I want to attend."

I continued angling, if only to be helpful.

"Oh, well, I'll get a taxi and take you there."

"I stay at La Maison Canadienne," she answered, "and it's out of your way."

She paused before crossing the street. A really old French car with a bad muffler whipped by, stopping us at the curb and for some reason reminding me of the Paris scenes in *Casablanca* (a film classic of which I own a 16mm print, by the way). When it was quiet again, Lisa stressed her point.

"And besides, at La Maison Canadienne, we don't allow visitors in our rooms."

Okay, so I had filed Maison Canadienne away for a contingency plan. But that wouldn't do me any good for right then.

"Listen, I'm leaving Paris tomorrow afternoon," I said, loving the sound of my World War II dialogue. "How will I ever see you again?"

I was totally unprepared for what happened next.

She kissed me. I felt her lips and the rain together.

"You'll find a way," she said, and went down into the Métro station.

Chapter

2

"OKAY, give me some fear! C'mon, you're gonna get hit! Jump!"

Wesley Crouch, the director, was screaming from the roof of the camera car as it came toward me. I did what I thought was right—jumped—and got screamed at again.

"Goddammit, Mike, you're going to get hit by this fucking car. Get fucking scared!"

It was already ten o'clock and Lisa hadn't shown up yet. Her meeting was supposed to be over by now. I had called her really early at La Maison Canadienne and told her we'd be filming at the Parc de Monceau. It's a little city park so we could get streets and trees, and it's not hard to find. Besides, it wasn't like we were going to be there all day. I looked over the bunch of people who were watching the filming out of curiosity. We had strung a rope and had a couple of gendarmes making sure no one got in our way.

The car came at me again, with Wesley screaming. I wondered if Laurence Olivier got started like this.

"Give it to me, Mikey, fear! Fear!"

I let out a yell and jumped to the side. The bastards almost really ran me down. Well, it was supposed to be a thriller.

"That's it! That's a take!" Wesley trumpeted.

At that moment I saw (she actually showed!) Lisa, wearing a hooded green leather coat, come walking up to the rope. She looked even better, if that's possible, than the night before. Of course I really couldn't give her more than a quick glance, since I was trying to pay attention to Wesley, who was explaining the next shot. After all, I was the star. I think she did manage to get in a little wave before I turned away, though.

The sequence Wesley was describing was one of those gray areas where I suppose I could have demanded a stunt man. Given I was lucky to be on this picture at all—and part of that was because I said I'd do the rough stuff—I figured I didn't have much room to squawk.

Wesley also took a moment to remind me I was playing the part of an ordinary guy who becomes involved in an international spy chase. He said that meant I shouldn't make anything look like an ordinary guy couldn't handle it. I told him not to worry.

I punctuated my reassurance with a huge sneeze and went scrounging through my pockets for a Kleenex. The romance of walking around Paris in the rain last night had left me with the beginnings of a cold.

Anyway, basically, I was supposed to jump in a car while it was moving, and take over the wheel from the guy who was driving.

The cameras were set up. It was time for the shot. Bob O'Connor, the line producer, helped position me. "Roll camera!" The car came down the street. Wesley screamed, "Action! Watch the goddamn car! Watch it!" (Jesus, I couldn't wait until we did more sync sound so I didn't have him screaming the whole goddamn time I'm acting.) Here came the car, nice and slow. Well, not that slow. I grabbed the door and opened it and jumped in the driver's side. There was an actor at the wheel. Another was in the rear seat. Both were playing the parts of enemy agents. The actor in the rear seat, a French bit player, grabbed my arm. That way I wouldn't fall back out. Wesley was shouting his head off at us. He had a bullhorn and I could barely understand him. Okay, get the wheel. "Karate chop! Goddammit!" I gave the driver a couple of punches and shoved him aside.

Crouch was running alongside the car.

"Cut! Goddammit! Cut!"

I stopped the car. How'd I do? Good?

"When I say hit him—hit the bastard!"

He ran back by the camera. The crew ran around getting everything set up again.

"Action!"

We went through the whole bit again. The cameraman loved it. Wesley wanted an insurance shot. One more time. We did it and it worked fine. At that point, I had a suggestion: Get a traveling shot of the action by having the camera car drive alongside.

Wesley commented thoughtfully on my idea.

"The worst. Putrid fucking idea. Forget it."

"Why?" I demanded. "Because you didn't think of it?"

"I thought of it and forgot it," Wesley maintained.

"It's just the kind of thing Ron Peters would like," I said.

That was playing dirty. Ron Peters was the executive producer and Big Boss over all of us. He was not with us on location, but he was the guy who cast me. Ron thought I had a lot of good ideas about the film. I always liked to invoke Ron's name when Wesley started giving me too much shit.

"I'll tell Ron you were thinking of him," Wesley said and walked away.

I went over and stood by the rope with my arms folded. Wesley and O'Connor and the cameraman had a quick meeting, after which O'Connor came up to me. He said they decided they would take a little time to film some different angles on the car—without me. He went back to Wesley.

I saw Lisa walking up to me from the crowd of onlookers.

"Hi," she said, smiling. She pushed the hood on the coat back and her hair showed gold in the sunlight.

"Hi," I said, not smiling. "Have you been here long?"

She ignored my question in favor of an observation on my rest period as perceived by a bystander. Namely, her.

"Gee, Michael, I'm really pleased you came over here, but aren't you supposed to be in front of the camera?"

Very clever. The girl knew nothing about the art of making motion pictures. I forgave her.

"They're getting some pickup shots," I explained.

She asked what that meant and I told her.

"Why did the director yell at you?" she asked sweetly.

Actually a number of directors get very excited during filming. I tried to explain that in lay terms.

"Because he's an asshole."

I called to O'Connor that since he was line producer he should start worrying about the sky clouding over if we didn't get moving. That really was none of my business, but I knew it would irritate the hell out of Wesley.

"Well, whatever the argument is, Michael, I'm on your side."

The sunlight made her eyes look even greener. I was having trouble concentrating.

"It's not an argument, Lisa. I'm just trying to do my job."

"And I gather it's not going too smoothly at the moment, right?"

Did she think this was a high school play?

"I just don't see why I have to resort to power plays to get the director to listen to me."

"Is standing over here a power play?" she asked.

"Well, I just reminded the director it was his boss, the exec producer, who wanted me in this picture."

O'Connor started waving for me to come over. It was time for another conference. Lisa wasn't finished with her inquiry.

"Think you'll have to make a power play with me?"

Okay, she wanted to kid around, fine. Just so she knows how much was on the line here.

"Listen, this picture only represents everything I've been working for all my life plus three million, eight hundred thousand bucks of other people's money!"

"Wow, Michael, all that money and I still feel funny about you paying for dinner," she said, and added: "Especially since I maneuvered you into asking me."

She what?

"Michael! Come on!" O'Connor screamed.

Why did I have to leave just when things were getting interesting? I wheeled around hoping to get in one more topper—not that I had one in mind—but Lisa had already gone back among the onlookers. I drifted over to O'Connor and Wesley to see what they wanted. Wesley was checking the sun; he was waiting for some clouds to pass.

Wesley took me through what I was supposed to do. Where it netted out was I would jump out of a Jaguar sedan while it was moving and it would crash and explode. There was a pile of cardboard and mattresses for me to land on.

I looked over the small crowd for Lisa. She was talking to one of the gendarmes. Is that what she had come here for? To practice her French? Well, at least she was staying out of my way. I mean, guests can be very distracting when you're trying to concentrate. Although, Christ, most people never even get to see a film being made. You'd think she could pay a little more attention.

Eddie Samuels, the special-effects guy, showed me how the car was rigged to explode. He would take care of that part with a radio control unit.

"Be sure to pull the wheel over toward those trees before you jump," Eddie told me.

"Okay, let's go! This is costing money!" bellowed Wesley.

As I got in the Jaguar, I inadvertently gave a quick look-see to check if Lisa were watching. She not only was, she actually waved to me. I gave her a little nod of the head (no harm in making her feel special; I did ask her to come out here) and started the engine up.

"Action!"

I started driving the car down the street. The door was open. Jesus, it seemed way too fast. Here came the mattresses. Wesley was screaming for me to jump.

No fucking way was I going to do this.

"Cut, goddammit!"

I stopped the car and got out. Wesley and Bob O'Connor came running over. What could I say? I blew it.

Wesley was kind. Too kind.

"Hey, no sweat, Mike baby, we'll have one of the stunt men take the fall."

He walked away with a big shit-eating grin on his face. I wandered back by the makeup man, Jerry Turner, for a touchup. Wesley made sense. It was a very difficult trick. Well, it wasn't that difficult—if I hadn't misjudged the speed of the goddam car—but definitely not worth getting hurt over. That's a bunch of bullshit about a lot of stars doing their own stunt work, anyway. I understood Clint Eastwood does some of his own stunt work, but he's an exception.

"Did something just go wrong?"

It was Lisa. She had convinced the gendarme she knew me and he had let her through the rope.

"You could say that," I said, watching Wesley go over the scene with the stunt man.

"Is that man going to take your place?"

I suppose I could have explained why it didn't matter. But the fact was, I didn't like the idea of Wesley's thinking I'd crapped out. Besides, I had been through a dry run so I knew what to do now. I looked at Lisa. I guess I'm a fool for green eyes.

"Not if I can help it," I said.

I started walking out to Wesley.

"You can do it, Michael," Lisa called after me. "I know you can."

Wesley did not want to take the time to give me another chance. I told him it would use up less time than standing around arguing about it. I got back in the car and started out. I'm not even sure if I waited for Wesley to say "Action." The door was open. The mattresses were coming up fast. I aimed the car toward the trees and jumped. Whomp! I hit the mattresses and rolled. I came up in time to see the car jump the curb. There was a moment when everything froze. Then it hit a tree. There was a big explosion and the car disappeared in flames. Shithouse mouse! Even the trunk lid flew into the air.

O'Connor was running toward me. The crew and all the people watching were applauding. Wesley even came over and told me it went great. O'Connor started shaking my hand. I looked at Lisa and gave her a little salute. She did the same in return, with a big beautiful smile following.

Now it was just a matter of a couple of closeups and we could all split back to the Ritz. We had to be on the plane to Scotland that afternoon, so I figured I only had a couple of hours to capitalize on the impression I had made on this impressionable young girl.

Lisa was plenty wound up from the filming. "Did you see that sucker *explode?*" she squealed. Unfortunately, the excitement of the moment was not enough to carry Lisa up to my room while I finished packing. That's okay. (It wasn't okay, but I didn't have much to say about it.) What ticked me off most was having to leave altogether. I mean, I was just getting to know her and wouldn't you know it? I had to leave. Well, it wouldn't be the first time business would interfere with my pleasure. Or the last. Anyway, O'Connor had said we'd come back for a few days to do interiors.

I went up and started packing, leaving Lisa in the lobby.

A little background. You have to understand that every picture, particularly a location job, is a kind of traveling small town. Which means the cast and the crew are rife with cliques and gossip and petty politics. But I was here, in incredible hotels, and getting some big money—so what the hell?

All this didn't come easy. There was the hustling: talking "projects" at the pool of the Beverly Hills Hotel and making sure I got next to the "right" people. Oh, and above all, listening to my agent.

The day my agent told me, I saw everybody at the Studio Grill. The news had preceded me.

"Michael, I hear they gave you the world."

"Not the world, Sammy, just a part. The lead."

We actors would always sit together and talk over the deals being made around the studios. Who's doing what, and to whom, and Gary's leaving for location, and Jeannie's signed for a series. Now I was making it, becoming an elite member of a very special group. I remembered fighting for an agent ("Don't you know there are a million talented people trying to break in?"), and eating Franco-American spaghetti twice a day, and scamming food when I could crash somebody's houseparty, and finally my first bit part in a made-for-TV movie. It was the start. Now here I was, in the starring role of a feature with locations in Paris, Scotland, and Morocco. What's next?

The phone rang. Lisa getting impatient?

"Hi, Michael, you still in your room?"

The voice was Bambi Perlmutter's. Bambi was production assistant in charge of everything somebody else wasn't in charge of. She was calling from Glasgow, Scotland, where she was making advance arrangements.

"I'm trying to get packed and leave for Scotland," I told her. "What do you want?"

She laughed.

"Two things, Michael. A, publicity. And B, more publicity."

I was standing there trying to listen and find the other half of a pair of socks at the same time.

"I just arranged for a reporter from *L'Express* to come over to the Ritz and talk with you."

She was trying to do a little extra. I decided to be nice.

"Hey, great, Bambi, if he shows soon I can give him something."

That was good by Bambi. All she wanted was for me to know she had made an effort. Which was something for a gal who was basically a gopher. (A gopher is someone who you have *go for* things. Coffee, air tickets, that kind of stuff.) Really, I wanted to do what I could to push the picture. Besides, it was in my contract. I could see myself at a press conference at the Plaza—no, make that the Sherry-Netherland. All the New York critics are there. . . .

Mother Fletcher! I've got Lisa downstairs. Why the hell couldn't Bambi say for me to stay in Paris? I checked around the room to make sure nothing was forgotten. The phone rang again. This time it was the desk telling me the reporters were there. I told them to get somebody up for my bags.

No special excitement in the lobby. Shit, just one reporter. A woman, and no camera. What the hell kind of interview was that? Oh, she did have a photographer. I got myself set for the pictures, wondering if French reporters would ask any more intelligent questions than American ones. Sure, I know we need them, but don't you think they need us?

"How did you prepare for this role, Monsieur Shym-kus?"

"I showered, shaved, and brushed my teeth."

"Monsieur?"

I made up something about researching counterespionage and that kind of stuff. And all the time I was checking the lobby for Lisa. Would she have ditched me after all this?

"Excuse me, please," I said. "I have to catch a plane."

I started toward the door. She must have bugged out on me. Shit!

"Psssssssst!"

It was Lisa, sitting behind a newspaper, just peeping over the top with her beautiful eyes. She waited!

"Lisa."

"Listen, big shot, I've only been sitting here practically a half-hour."

I took her hand, because let's be honest about it, I wanted to touch her.

"I'm sorry. Really."

Was it my imagination or did she just squeeze my hand?

"What was all that going on over there?" she asked.

"A reporter for *L'Express.*"

A squeeze. Definitely.

"Wow! You're famous."

"I'm working on it."

She stood up and put the paper down. We both noticed the reporter and her cameraman looking at us.

"Hey, Lisa, do you want to have your picture taken with me?"

"Absolutely not," she insisted.

Just to make sure I didn't try any tricks, she gave a pull on my hand and led me out to the street. There were plenty of people and cars. A gendarme on a bicycle went by.

"You missed your big chance, Lisa."

"Oh, no, Michael, you're the actor," she cautioned me. "When I do something, it's for real."

"Like your kiss last night?"

"Well . . ."

"Well?"

If I have anything, it's a natural sense of timing. It was time. I put my arms around Lisa, there, in front of the Ritz. We kissed. It was good. Very good. And long. We finished, finally, but we would not let go of each other.

"Listen, Michael, I don't like the way you're running things."

Oh, no. I've messed up somehow.

"What should I do different?"

"Stay in Paris."

I held on tight. Life was being extremely unfair.

"I had better warn you," I started.

"About what?"

"I think I'm coming down with a cold."

"Don't worry, Michael, I'll survive," she said softly to encourage me.

We kissed again. I thought, I've got a hundred-and-fifty-dollar-a-day room upstairs and I'm out on the street. Forget it. I wasn't complaining. Not with Lisa.

The bellman came out with my bags and patiently stood by. I decided to restablish my domination.

"Okay, Lisa, I'm off."

She kind of stood there, looking at me but not saying anything. The doorman had a cab come up.

"I do have to get to Scotland, you know," I said.

She spoke at last. I'm sure I saw her bite her lip.

"Yeah, well, Michael, nice seeing you and all that."

"Yes," I agreed, "maybe we'll run into each other again sometime."

The cab was behind me with the door open. I started to get in, then turned back to her.

"By the way, Lisa, there's a possibility we'll be coming back to Paris. Would you mind terribly if the instant I get to Scotland tonight I let you know my plans?"

Chuckling to myself, I started to get in the cab without waiting for an answer. I got her reply anyway.

"Only on one condition," she began.

"What?" I practically squeaked, totally unable to keep concern out of my voice.

"That your plans include me."

I sat down and looked up at her. Things were back on course.

"Now, now, Lisa. I thought you don't like it when I take charge."

She leaned in close to me. Her soft hair came forward and framed her face.

"Yes I do."

I spent the whole ride to Orly airport trying to decide whether I really came out ahead in that exchange.

It turned out Wesley and O'Connor had taken earlier flights. When I got to Glasgow there was a message for me at the British Airways desk.

Michael,

We've decided to check locations outside of Inverness. See you tonight at the New Caledonian Hotel.

Bob

P.S. We're taking the train to get a feel for the landscape.

Christ! As if Glasgow wasn't far enough north. I tried to comfort myself by recalling we would be in Morocco in a couple of weeks, but that didn't do a thing for my cold. Okay, I split for the railway station and took the train north to Inverness. It was a pretty landscape. You could see rabbits running for hedgerows. There were fat, woolly sheep in meadows. Every once in a while I'd spot an old castle ruin, too.

At times there was also light snow falling. The idea was to get to Scotland and film before the weather got any worse. Big deal. I was feeling shittier by the minute—sore throat, stopped-up nose, the works. Oh, me. What if I don't kick this before we make the move to Morocco?

When I saw Bambi in the lobby of the New Caledonian Hotel, I immediately hit her up for some Kleenex.

"Welcome to Inverness. Bob and Wesley are in the bar," she volunteered, staring at me.

"What are you looking at?" I asked. (Which came out, "Wad are you looging ad?")

"You're really pale, Michael."

After Bambi told me what she knew about our scheduled return to Paris, I sent my bags up to my room and went into the little bar off the lobby. Bob and Wesley were seated on a sofa in the back, comparing scotches.

"Here's to me good pal, Michael," said Wesley, raising his glass.

"Aye, to Michael-me-boy's good health," said Bob, giving his best Scottish imitation.

I replied with a sneeze.

"This fresh, clear, cold, icy Scottish air will be clearin' up those sniffles, me lad," Wesley claimed.

Something told me I was being jived. How wonderful it is to be with people who are truly concerned about you.

"It's nothing," I said, not very convincingly. "Just a little cold."

"That's what you get for sticking your bare ass up in the air all night," my director said, causing O'Connor to giggle.

"Eat your heart out," I retorted, causing O'Connor to laugh.

"Get some rest." Wesley snorted. "I'd hate to have to edit you out."

"Actually," I said, "I'm looking forward to a nice warm bed."

"There's no heat," Bob said. Wesley Crouch convulsed in laughter.

"You've gotta be kidding me."

They weren't. My room was strictly the pits. An old wooden dresser, a squeaky bed, and an open window with snow coming in. Ah, the glamour of stardom.

I shut the window on the snow and got into my

pajamas. It wasn't near warm enough, so I put a sweater on, too. That done, I called Lisa.

After I worked my way through the overseas operator, a woman at La Maison Canadienne answered, speaking French.

"Parlez-vous anglais?" I asked.

Now there's a really dumb question. If she understood English, why ask in French? And if she didn't, I was out of luck, anyway.

"Oui, yes."

"Is Lisa Foster there, please?"

It was a ten-minute wait for Lisa. I reminded myself to call person-to-person next time. Assuming there was a next time.

Finally, Lisa picked up the phone.

"Hello?"

I imagined her in Paris, as I had first seen her through the café window.

"Hi, Lisa."

"Michael, is that you?"

Her voice was beautiful, too.

"Who else?" I said, then, afraid she might give me a list of possibilities, I quickly added, "Just me."

"You sound terrible," she said.

What a downer. How can you be romantic with a cold?

"I'm up to my neck in English Kleenex."

"You can do your own stunt work, but you can't take a little rain, right?" she teased.

I told her what Bambi had said. That it looked like we'd get back to Paris for more filming after we finish in Morocco. Lisa sounded excited, but we both felt it seemed a long way off. We made small talk about the restaurant, La Méditerranée. She told me her friends at La Maison Canadienne were really knocked out that I'd taken her to such an expensive place. I told her it was nothing, really. She went into a report on some sixteenth-century tapestries about a unicorn at a museum she went to. I told her about the train ride. She mentioned she was going to work on a political campaign for one of her teachers. He wanted to run for the municipal council of Paris. Sounded interesting. Anyway, her voice was great medicine.

"Okay, Li, if you don't hear from me, I've been found frozen in my room."

"When you come back to Paris I promise to keep you warm."

Oh-oh.

"You're making it really hard to get off the phone."

"Golly, Michael, I can't put anything over on you."

"But I do have to say goodnight."

"Go ahead. I can take it."

"Goodnight—and remember," I lowered my voice, "that I'm crazy about you."

"Yeah, I figured you're either crazy," she thought a moment, "or handing out a line of crap."

What? I need this?

"Okay, Lisa. Goodnight."

"Michael?"

"Yeah?"

"Will you please call me sometime soon so I can decide?"

"About what?"

"Whether it's a line or insanity."

Okay. So maybe I didn't have enough sense to come out of the rain. But I think I just got Lisa to ask me to call her.

Chapter

3

THE filming in Scotland almost finished me.

After a week freezing in Inverness, Wesley decided
we should move to Inveraray—a teeny little village in
the Scottish highlands—for a more rugged location. By
this time, I was already coughing a lot. A rational
person would have stayed put, right? But it was for
art, so I went. Here was my plan: do the sequences in
Inveraray, then stay inside for a day or two and rest.

Wesley must have had a plan, too. Namely, to do me
in.

We had a six-a.m. call for the first day's shooting in
Inveraray. It was still dark as we drove twenty miles
out to the location—some stone ruins by a creek. Wesley
went over the action with me and Heather Lynch, a
Scottish actress they had brought in. The idea was that
Heather and I were running from enemy agents. She
gets captured and I escape. Seemed simple enough.

When there was enough light, we started filming. Let
me go on record as saying Scotland in the fall is not your
ideal weather for outdoor moviemaking. It was windy.
And cold! And there were off-and-on rain showers.

Okay, the show goes on. "Action!" We set off running alongside the creek. Exciting stuff, with lots of special-effects explosions set off all around. The air filled with clouds of fuller's earth from the blasting. Jesus! I was out of breath. Naturally, Wesley wanted a retake. We ran our asses off ten times. And everybody is screaming it looked good the first time.

When that was over I crawled into the van while they were out doing the closeups of Heather getting captured. Jerry Turner got out his makeup kit and started working on me. He was putting some fake cuts on. "Michael, I gotta tell you," he was saying, as he put some fake blood on my arm, "I think you're really too sick—you gotta back off."

My answer to that was cough, sneeze, and blow. What the hell did Jerry think I was supposed to do? My whole career had been to get me to this movie. So I had a cold. Tough. Although, I must say, O'Connor was really starting to worry. As line producer, he had to bring the movie in on time and within budget. Now he had a nightmare of me folding to contend with. Wesley was already talking (hell, he could hardly wait) about restructuring the story with less of me in it. Shit! If I could only shake this cold.

I looked out in the meadow, in front of the ruins, and saw a car being driven up. A group led by Wesley had gone over to meet it. The driver got out and opened the passenger side. A small blond woman got out. It was Eve.

(Should I be surprised? Naturally, Eve would show up if there were some big problem with me. Correction: Make that any problem.)

Eve was, is, Eve Ross: agent provocateur. Eve built me (which is strictly her version; she picked me up after I got started doing bit parts) and made me rich (also her story; I am not that rich, yet, although she did get me—and herself through me—a lot more money than I ever dreamed I could get). So now here was Eve. Right in the middle of the shoot. To get me straightened out.

Welsey was doing a lot of yelling and waving his arms around. He kept pointing over to me. Not that Eve would look. What a bunch of crap. Here were fifty people shut down so Wesley could get his two cents in with Eve. Well, it must be pretty serious if they called Eve to fly over. I mean, can you imagine? Now she can try to take credit once more for everything I do.

"I've actually got them to sign you for this picture, Michael."

"No kidding. My talent didn't have a thing to do with it, right, Eve?"

"Talent's just a beginning, Michael." .

"Eve, if you're so terrific, why don't you get into acting?"

"I would—if I had me for an agent."

So what difference did Eve make, really? A lot. Nobody said no to Eve Ross. She was a smart, conniving, tenacious, fierce woman. And usually right—the bitch.

Fortunately for me, she was on my side. She was out making the calls, hitting the parties, putting the deals together. (She was so well connected, she actually got the executive producer of this picture to throw her a "surprise" fortieth birthday party.) Of course, I wasn't her only "property," as she was probably reminding herself at this very moment. There were a top screenwriter, a few well-chosen name actors, and two important directors. And me, who might finally make it and pay off big. All for and because of Eve Ross, who had a million things to do and much talent to handle and deals to make and papers to sign. Yet, she has to get on a plane and come all the way to England because one of *her* people is in trouble.

God, did I ever dream of getting another agent or crossing her in any way? Did I ever!

The group parted and Wesley and Eve came sauntering over to me. I got down out of the van and Eve gave me a big hug. "You look just fine, Michael. Now please cooperate with Wesley." I told Eve how happy I was she could get away to visit us. After this perfunctory gushiness, Wesley explained the scene to me. I was supposed to run beside the creek. There would be an explosion. At that point, I would escape by jumping in the creek. Creek? What's with this creek jazz? I mean, like it's freezing and I'm supposed to go in the water? With my cold? I told Wesley he could take a flying leap at a rolling doughnut. He looked over at Eve. Okay, what about the stunt man? Wesley said he needed the closeups and this wasn't really stunt work.

Now don't think I won't take risks. Look what I did in Paris. And once in Hong Kong I drove a car into the side of a building (I did take a stunt course, I'll admit), and another time in Kobe, Japan, I jumped from a freighter into the harbor—about forty feet. But at that time I wasn't dying of a cold.

Eve didn't say a word. She just nodded yes to me one time, slowly.

Everything was set up. The cameras were going. I ran along the bank of the creek. Explosion. I jumped. I got out and did it again. This time they had me stay in the water for closeups. Jesus, it was freezing. I started shaking.

Wesley wanted to do some more. My head was spinning. I literally couldn't breathe. O'Connor came over and I reached up so he could help me out. On the bank, I caught my breath enough to gasp:

"You gotta get me out of here."

Back at the George Hotel in Inveraray, I sat in front of a coal fire waiting for a ride into Glasgow. I wasn't cold any more. In fact, I was sweating. Jerry Turner brought me some blankets and was telling anyone who would listen he had warned me I wasn't taking care of myself. Bambi was a lot more useful. She brought me some chicken soup. There was no regular doctor in the village (thank God, I could have gotten stuck there), and besides, everyone thought I should go to a hospital in Glasgow. Shit on that! Glasgow looked gray and drab and cold when I was there. I figured it was the last place to get laid up in the hospital. Besides, no way was I going into a hospital if I had anything to say about it. I hate hospitals. What I wanted was to get to a nice warm hotel in London.

I pulled the blankets around my shoulders like a benched football player. Why the hell did I have to get sick now? My big break, everything going right, and now I'm on my way out. This could cost a fortune in production money, although we were pretty much finished with this sequence, and even more, it could cost me the picture. Big deal. A lot of good the picture would do me if I'm dead.

Wesley Crouch and O'Connor came in and sat opposite me. I just stared at them. Wesley told me not to worry. He could go ahead and do the rest of the Scottish stuff without me. He said he was also rewriting the script, just in case. Terrific. I was too weak to argue with him. Wesley made a remark about being sickly and left. Bob told me to call him as soon as I saw a doctor. I went back to staring at the fire.

Bambi stuck her head in the room.

"We've got a film reviewer from Boston here. Can you see him a second?"

I sneezed loudly in response.

She left but I was not to be alone.

"Michael doll, are you still alive?" queried the voice of my agent. Of course that's the first thing Eve Ross would want to know—whether she could still count on getting her percentage.

"Barely," I replied. "You here to finish me off?"

"Listen, I didn't come all the way from Los Angeles to argue with you," she said, handing me a fresh Kleenex from her Hermès bag.

"What, then?"

"Wesley has been calling Ron Peters and saying he could replace you by making some plot changes."

So he really does hate me.

"Sure I'm sick," I admitted, "but what Wesley's worried about is me getting more credit for this film than he does."

She waved me off.

"Forget that—he's just trying to finish the film. Besides, it's up to Peters, and I can hold him if you get well."

"Thanks, Eve," I said begrudgingly, and held out my hand for another Kleenex.

"Now what do you want to do?" she asked, adjusting the oversize glasses she only wore indoors.

"Go to London and see a doctor and do whatever the hell he says."

Bambi came in. She announced to Eve that everything was confirmed.

"Oh, now that you've settled this," I said, "I suppose you're heading home?"

"No," Eve replied, "that's *our* reservations for London."

Great. Eve was coming with me. Was there no cure that would rid me of her?

Dr. Poole's office was on Basil Street, right near Harrods department store. The good doctor was a dead ringer for Rex Harrison. He worked me over with a cold stethoscope, and awarded me a "Congratulations, you have a very serious bronchitis, just about to go into pneumonia." He started to write out a prescription for penicillin. I informed him I was allergic to the stuff. (I knew that would catch up with me one day, but I never dreamed it would be for this.) He switched me to Septrin, twice a day for seven days, and lots of rest. He also promised me I could make it to Morocco. I expressed my gratitude and my doubt. Outside, I wandered around for twenty minutes to find a chemist's (that's British for drugstore) to get the pills.

At last, I got in a taxi.

"The Churchill Hotel," I wheezed.

Allow me to introduce you to the Churchill. The Churchill Hotel is not your basic quaint little English hotel with drafty rooms and no heat. The Churchill is a Loew's hotel. The same Loew's which owns the Waldorf and Loew's Monte Carlo. The Churchill actually has individual thermostats in every room. And given the way I felt on that rainy night in London, I would have killed for a thermostat.

In my room, with the thermostat up and me under the covers, I prepared to crash. To experience total relaxation.

Knock-knock. It was Eve. She was there to "eat in" with me, so we could be alone. To "be alone" with Eve meant me, her, and the phone.

"I've got to get hold of Ron Peters at his office," she announced, trying to impress me by showing how easily she can just pick up the phone and talk to the executive producer.

"There's the phone," I said.

She pulled up a chair next to the bed, put the phone to her ear, and began talking to me.

"Think you'll be up for Morocco in a few days?"

"The doctor says yes."

"Ron? Is that you?" inquired Eve of the phone, as she began a thirty-five-minute conversation to California, looking at me the entire time. (She always looked at you when she talked to the phone—and at the phone while she talked to you.)

When she finished, she called room service and ordered supper.

"Now," she said, dialing her answering service in L.A., "where was I?"

"I dunno, you were talking to Ron."

"Yes, he's very upset about you being ill."

"Maybe someone can do a publicity article on me practically having pneumonia," I said, figuring I could get Eve to think about real life for a moment.

"I like that," Eve commented, without missing a beat, "a whole production shut down because of one man—a star."

"Wait a minute," I said, realizing she had taken me seriously.

"Just think," she went on, "it really would make you seem like a star."

I still wasn't sure of her intent.

"Maybe we can get a puff in the *Journal of the American Medical Association,*" I suggested.

She began dialing another number. (There was always another number.) As I heard the rings, she added, "But then, I don't want people to get the idea you're sickly." I decided I could put my time to better use by going into the bathroom and taking my pill.

The food arrived and Eve had the cart put near the phone. (That was a switch, anyway; she usually had the phone brought to her table.) The bellman mixed us a Caesar salad while I started on some tomato soup with croutons. When he left, Eve began our "talk."

For tonight's lecture, she picked her "do I have to do everything myself?" speech. The topic—which can be adjusted to fit any occasion or transgression—revolved around her having to leave her other people in Los Angeles (they should send me a statement of gratitude) and come here to straighten things out herself. Even my own mother, who lives happily with my father in Chicago, could never make me feel as low as Eve could. Wisely, I responded to none of this harangue. I just pigged out happily on the duck *à l'orange* and mixed vegetables, and more than my share of Médoc wine.

Deciding she had made me feel sufficiently indebted for her efforts to earn her percentage of my income, she changed to standard subject C, or Career. Specifically, my career.

"Michael, as soon as this wraps, I think I can get you into something very good."

"At the moment, Eve, I'm only concentrating on staying alive."

"Just in case you do, we've got to look ahead."

That, I took it, was not optimism, but a command.

"What's the deal?" I asked, wearily (as well as warily).

"Ron Peters is still so high on you . . ." she paused, and then added with flourish, "he'd like to have you in his next feature with one of my directors."

"C'mon, Eve." I cut myself off with enough of a sneeze to make her move her plate of stuffed capon breast. "I don't want to be packaged with your other people."

"I only package the best," insisted Eve, adding pointedly, "mostly."

"What's that supposed to mean?" I inquired, really getting perturbed.

"That means I'm very tired from jet lag, Michael."

"Okay, let's drop it."

"You can go over the script to see how you like it," she offered.

"Eve, if it's okay with you, it's okay with me." Wait a minute. Did I just give her the right to decide on the script?

"Well, I think it's super," she said. Translation: They're interested in my playing the lead.

Was that the end of my Career discussion? Hah! As if acting offers were all there were to my career.

"Are you still dating that girl?" she asked, in the way of innocent social conversation.

"What girl?" I responded, trying to figure out if she had anyone particular in mind.

"Carol Benson," she informed me. "She's so lovely, wouldn't you say?"

"I would if I could remember what she looks like." Carol Benson, Carol Benson. Oh, yeah, she went with me to a reception in Bel Air last spring. A lot of the biggies were there. I couldn't remember if she left with me or went home with friends. But why her, of all girls?

"She's going to be a regular in a TV series," Eve went on, "and a picture of you two did show up in the press."

"Really?" I said. "I didn't know *Dog World* covered the party circuit."

"Her father is Sam Fisher, one of our most successful producers," Eve said. "I'd say she's company worth keeping."

"No kidding," I said flatly.

The phone rang. It was for Eve.

*   *   *

The evening ended with Eve still on the phone, calling the hotel operator to find out what time it was.

"I really must get some sleep, Michael," she said, going out the door.

Eve was leaving for New York in the morning. Now you might think someone who had flown straight through from Los Angeles to Glasgow earlier that day would at least want to rest a few days, or maybe even stick around and see something. But that would imply that something could get along without Eve, and we couldn't have that. She could be in New York by tomorrow night. Perhaps have supper with a television programming exec. Nobody could say Eve was harder on her "talent" than she was on herself. Still, she was plenty hard on us "talent." But you did what she said and you got where you were supposed to go. I can attest to that.

Goddammit, anyway.

In the hopes of getting to sleep on a better note, I picked up the phone (still warm) and called Lisa.

She had just gotten in from a meeting for the political campaign she was working on and really fell out when I told her I had bronchitis, practically pneumonia. I also threw in the part about getting over it in seven days. (She was as skeptical as I was about that.) The next thing I laid on her was my big idea to detour through Paris on my way to Morocco, assuming I went to Morocco. That she liked, but worried about me trying to do too much before I was well. She asked about the ranting and raving and various machinations between me and the director. I told her. She said it sounded pretty interesting after a day studying about Charles Maurras and the turn-of-the-century right-wing party Action française.

"So Wesley Crouch is stuck waiting until you show up in Morocco?" she asked.

"Yeah," I said. "Do you think I should let them rewrite without me, so they can start?"

"No, Michael, make that bastard squirm. You deserve to enjoy yourself now."

Dear, sweet Lisa.

"Baby," I said, "You're my kind of girl."

Chapter

4

FIVE days later I landed at Orly airport, only slightly out of my way to Casablanca. First, I checked on my afternoon flight out. That done, I wended my way through all the people running around and called La Maison Canadienne for Lisa.

"Yes, Monsieur Shymkus, you're to meet Lisa at the top of the Eiffel Tower."

Terrific. She was supposed to wait in her room. I had about four hours in Paris and she wanted to go sightseeing. I wondered how windy it would be up there. What the hell? According to Dr. Poole I was supposed to be well in two days. But I was still coughing. He was shipping me off to Morocco, uncured.

"You sure I'll be okay, Doc?"

"Mr. Shymkus, go to Morocco, make your movie, and get laid."

Veddy civilised, these British.

Not that *that* wasn't on my mind. I mean, hell, why not? Of course, I only had four hours. Let's see, figuring cab rides, the elevator to the top of the Eiffel Tower and back down—no, it'd never work.

Occupied by these lofty thoughts, I started for the taxi stand. On my way there a man, middle-aged, came up to me.

"Excuse me," he said in pure Midwest American, "but it's for my daughter."

Sounded intriguing.

"Right." Beat, beat. "What's for your daughter?"

"The autograph."

He waved and I saw what were obviously the wife and daughter coming over.

"Are you sure I am who you think I am?" I asked quickly.

The girl, who looked about fifteen, replied with confidence.

"You're Michael Shymkus. I saw you on television."

All right. So I was flattered. I mean, here I was in an airport in France and people want my autograph. I asked her name—Mary Beth—and wrote on a page of her guidebook: *To Mary Beth, always, Michael Shymkus.*

"I couldn't believe it when Mary Beth said it was you," Mary Beth's mom said. "Wait'll we show the other people on the charter."

"Are you on vacation, sir?" asked her dad.

Loving every moment, I let them have it.

"No, I'm on my way to Morocco to do a movie."

What an asshole thing to say, even though it was true. Their only appropriate response was, "Wonderful."

They apologized for stopping me. As I started away, Mary Beth took another look at the autograph and said, "Thank you, Mr. Shymkus."

That did it. I walked back up to them and said, "No, I thank you, Mary Beth."

Then I ran for a cab.

"Eiffel Tower, *s'il vous plaît.*"

I was curious why Lisa hadn't waited until I called.

Okay, the main thing was getting some time with her. Soon I could see the Eiffel Tower. The driver managed not to get too tangled up in traffic. Still, there was your basic Parisian hornblowing and shouting. When he let me off, he showed me to the fast elevator at the north base. I got my ticket and zipped to the top.

As it turned out it was an unusually warm day for the season, which was a lucky break for me. There were plenty of people, tourists from all over—Japanese, Americans, Germans, various others.

And Lisa. She saw me the same moment I saw her. The wind was blowing, lifting her hair. And all Paris was behind her. She was wearing these nifty tight-fitting bright-blue corduroy overalls that really showed how long her legs were, and a yellow sweater and a knit scarf.

"Hi," Lisa said.

"Hi."

We looked at each other, smiling.

"Lisa," I said, "I've got a really dumb thing to tell you."

"Okay."

Why do these things happen to me?

"Well, we shouldn't kiss," I warned her. "I'm not supposed to be well for two more days."

"Who says I was going to kiss you, el sicko?"

Oh, boy. I was trying to look out for her health and I'd only insulted her.

"Well, I just—"

"But I do want to hug you, Michael. Real bad."

We put our arms around each other. Tight. I could feel Lisa's body and it was firm and, well, giving, against my chest. There seemed to be only us. And the sky. And Paris. I'm not sure a kiss would have meant what holding her meant. Not just then, anyway. Besides, it was so typical something would keep us apart.

"You don't look sick to me," she said.

"I don't feel too bad, either," I answered, "but I'm taking no chances."

She took my hand.

"Okay, no chances," she repeated.

She pointed out the curving arms of the Palais de Chaillot. There was a red carpet up the steps and black Citroëns were pulling up for some dignitary. Big deal. The most important thing in Paris was happening up here.

I wondered where she was when I called.

"Hey, Lisa, I thought you were going to wait for me at La Maison Canadienne."

She looked hurt.

"You don't like the view."

"I love it," I said, and looking at her, added, "particularly what's in front of it."

She walked me to the other side.

"Actually, I had to stop at the Sorbonne this morning. It's all for that project helping one of the profs campaign for a vacant seat on *le conseil municipal*," she said. "You see, I spent yesterday afternoon and last night talking with Claude and missed turning in a petition."

She sure slipped that Claude (she pronounced it "Clewed") thing in nice and neat.

"Oh, how'd you do?"

What I really wanted to know was how Claude did.

"Fine," she said. "We got six hundred signatures and Professor Thomer was thrilled. I know he'd be a good *conseiller*."

Can you believe it? I mean, am I an idiot? The election jazz is a front. She's got some guy named Claude she spends her nights with, while I am flying way the hell out of my way—practically with pneumonia, mind you—and feeling lucky to hug her.

Shit!

"Is everything set for Morocco?" Lisa asked.

No doubt she was trying to change the subject.

"I suppose."

"Aren't you going there this afternoon?"

Jesus! She couldn't wait to get rid of me.

"Yeah, I'm going, Lisa. Probably be tied up for two or three weeks, maybe longer."

"Are you still coming back here?"

"I dunno."

Might as well ease out of it now. Bye-bye, Lisa. Or is there a reason I was supposed to come popping back into Paris? The amazing thing is she had told me about a Philippe Budin, a civil engineering student who had paid her a lot of attention to no avail. And it was no secret about this campaign for Thomer. But for sure she didn't tell me nothing about no Claude, who she's really rolling around with. Well, what she does is her business. Son of a bitch! I'd just like about five minutes alone with this guy.

"Seems like you'll be in Morocco a long time," she said, sounding honestly disappointed.

"That's the way it is."

"Yes, of course, what's the matter with me?" she said, taking my arm and showing me another view. This time Montmartre, with the sun reflecting off the white Church of Sacré Coeur.

I was having a hard time concentrating on the sights. What I was really doing was brooding over the change my life had just taken.

Lisa must not have picked up on my mood.

"I was telling Claude about you and the film. . . ." she started.

That did it!

"Hey!" I barked. "I'm not interested in hearing about

Claude, and I'm sure Claude isn't interested in hearing about me!"

Lisa turned away from the view with a disturbed look on her face.

"But she is too."

"She?"

The look on Lisa's face changed. A smile came with realization. And laughter. And a hug.

"You've got some really tacky thoughts, Michael."

"Well, what am I supposed to think? I mean, Claude is a guy's name, and besides . . ."

"C'mon." She took my arm. "Let's go down and see the park here."

"So you maintain Claude is a female," I said, with the air of a cross-examiner.

We were walking in the Champ de Mars, the park in front of the Eiffel Tower.

"She's not only a female, she's sixty-one years old."

Claude Saché was the *directrice* at La Maison Canadienne. She was a kind of housemother, and especially she was Lisa's friend. That's what Lisa maintained, anyway; being a good amateur psychologist, I maintained Claude was a mother substitute. As it was, we got into all this by Lisa's telling me how when she first came to Paris she had no place to stay. I remarked I was surprised her mother let her travel with no set arrangements. That brought out the whole story about her folks. I did remember her saying something during one of our phone calls about losing her father when she was just a little girl. (It seems her dad was a captain in the Canadian army, and he was killed in a training accident when she was only seven.) She and her mother went to live in a little town called Constance Bay, in the province of Ontario. It was just across the river from the province of Quebec. After high school, Lisa went away to college in Ottawa, which is the capital. During her junior year her mother got cancer of the liver. Lisa went home to stay with her mother until she died. Then she decided to take the insurance (which gave her a little to live on every month) and study French politics at the Sorbonne. Her first room had been in a terrible cheap hotel, with Algerians scratching at her door at night, asking if she was lonely. At the university, she naturally met some other Canadians and found out about La Maison Canadienne. It was definitely inexpensive, a major prerequisite. From that followed the meeting with Claude and lots of Claude's motherly (or if you prefer Lisa's version, friendly) advice and comfort.

"Now who, in your sweet trashy mind," she asked after that rambling explanation, "did you think Claude was?"

I sure didn't want to go into that.

"Nobody," I said nonchalantly.

"Don't you have somebody you turn to for advice?"

"Sure I do."

"Well, who, then?"

I wasn't sure I wanted to get into that, either.

"It's a woman, too, as a matter of fact."

Now it was Lisa's turn to get suspicious.

"I was afraid of that, Michael," she said and I saw her eyes go down.

"Well, don't be."

We stopped while a child pedaled by in a little wooden horse and buggy. There were other children pedaling the same colorful contraptions around. Their nurses and fashionably dressed Parisian mothers were watching them.

"You don't have to tell me if you don't want to," Lisa offered.

"Good. Let's drop it," I said.

"What's her name?" Lisa asked.

"Eve Ross."

"Is she your best friend?"

"Honey," I said, "she's no friend at all."

"Well, are you two getting, are you now, or have you ever been, married?"

Now that tickled me. She thought I had something going, too. I figured it was time to tell her Hollywood isn't all glitter.

"No, nothing simple like marriage," I answered. "She's my agent."

"I'd say she's pretty lucky to be that."

"Nicely put, Li," I said. "But I'm not so lucky to be her client."

"She got you into this film, right?"

"Yeah, sure," I replied. "I had nothing to do with it."

She mulled that over for a little bit. Maybe it would get through to her what it meant to depend on an agent. To knock yourself out and build your easily shattered confidence from rejection so you can keep calling yourself an actor. Then, just when you've proved yourself enough to get some decent parts, the credit for landing any work goes to the agent.

"Okay, so it's a two-way thing," she said. "What's the big deal?"

"My life."

"You wanna run that by me again, Mike?" she requested. "I think I'm having trouble with your American slang."

"The big deal is she's in charge of my entire life."

Lisa looked around to see if anyone was listening.

"Has she got something on you, Michael?"

"Come on, Lisa, I'm not *that* interesting," I said. "We're talking about becoming a success."

"So you let her tell you what to do to be successful," she decided. "Sounds okay to me."

"Not when it means telling me everything."

We sat down on a bench and I laid it out for her—what *everything* meant. Like where to live and how to dress. Who to date and where to take them. What parties to attend, what to say, and who to say it to. And having my picture taken with people I couldn't even stand, all to create a Michael Shymkus who didn't really exist.

"Oh, poor baby," she said with mock pity. "I can really tell you hate living in California and going to Europe to be in a movie and being a big star."

"I didn't say I was a big star," I protested, "I said I'm seeing now what it takes to get there—and I don't like it."

It amazed me that although I was arguing with Lisa I really felt closer to her. I mean, the things I was saying were so inside me I would never have told them to anyone else.

"Lisa, I don't know if it's Eve or if it's the whole goddamn movies," I went on, "but I wanted to act, and to her that's the least of what I do."

"Are you the only person she's an agent for?" she asked, her brow knitting just a little.

Ha! Now she would see just where I fit into all this.

"Hell, no," I said. "She's got other talent she represents—actors, writers, directors. I'm not the only one."

"She must know what she's doing," Lisa said.

"That's just the problem; she's doing it to me."

"Michael, I don't know diddly-squat about agents, but it sure sounds like she's getting you what you want."

"You're missing the whole goddamn point," I growled.

"But, if you didn't like it, wouldn't you get out?"

We had obviously come to an impasse. It occurred to me what we were dealing with was a really major difference in where we were coming from. I was a product of big-city and big-money America. Wide-open wheeler-dealer Hollywood itself. That meant a whole success system of going after something and doing whatever you have to do to get it. Lisa was small-town Canadian, nice and clean and northern. That had to be old-fashioned and straighter to begin with, right? And besides, even worse than that, she was in school. A pure person. *Ars gratia artis*. Idealism. Revolution. Just enough money to live poorly on. Bullshit! The world wasn't like that, but she would never buy it from me.

I figured out a way to show just how crass Eve was.

"Listen, Lisa, the only reason Eve came over when I got sick was to make sure nothing got screwed up with my job."

It backfired.

"You mean she left all her other business and flew to Scotland because you had a cold?"

"Bronchitis!"

She sat through some more reasons on why Eve was only concerned with getting her percentage, but it made no impression on her. I looked at my watch.

"Oh, Jesus! I've got to get to my plane," I said, jumping up. We hadn't gone to lunch or anything.

"Yeah, well, nice talking to you," she said, shaking my hand.

"C'mon, Lisa," I said. I started to kiss her, then, depriving myself in a display of incredible will power, embraced her instead.

She pulled back, put her hands on both sides of my face, and kissed me anyway.

"When will you be back?" she asked. Her eyes were big and worried.

"Soon," I replied. "That is, I hope."

"Here's hoping."

She kissed me again. Her lips were incredibly soft.

"Duty calls," I said, and took off running for a cab.

The Royal Air Morocco Caravelle stopped first in Tangiers, then flew on to Casablanca.

Everyone was staying at the Marhaba Hotel. It had overhead fans and guys in fezes. I could just imagine Sidney Greenstreet in one of the big straw chairs in the bar.

The next day there was plenty of hot sun, which was great. We filmed lots of stuff in the harbor, on ships. Wesley wasn't too bad, either, now that he realized I wasn't going to conveniently disappear. Two nights later I took my last pill and awaited the big relapse in the morning. Bless Dr. Poole. The morning after came not even a runny nose.

From Casablanca, we went up to Tangiers for another week and a half to finish the Moroccan scenes. When we finally wrapped, O'Connor told me to check with Bambi on the move to Paris. Those interior scenes were still on. For a change the movie was on my side.

It took the usual four hours to get through from Morocco to Paris. (Their phone system is the worst.) There was another fifteen-minute wait for Lisa. I hadn't talked with her for three days. Now I could tell her the news.

"Say, Lisa, I was just wondering if we, you know, might be able to get together in Paris sometime?"

"Sure, sometime."

"Like how's tomorrow afternoon at two?"

"Gee, I don't know."

Now what's she trying to pull?

"What I mean, Michael, is, can't you make it any sooner?"

Chapter

5

THE Chez Julien on the Rue St. Denis is a dynamite-looking restaurant.

Not necessarily dynamite-eating. But looking, definitely.

First off, it's got these really excellent *fin de siècle* designs. When you come in there's a huge curvy wooden bar. You can just imagine the days of the demimonde and Toulouse-Lautrec. There are murals, too—big, flowery women. And a ceiling skylight glowing with stained glass. You see, I took some art in college, too.

But the most beautiful part of the restaurant that day was Lisa.

The day really started with me getting into Paris and heading straight for the hotel. In a way, I guess I was kind of nervous about seeing Lisa. I mean, here I was back in Paris and we were going to see each other, which could lead to, well, seeing each other more. Now ordinarily, I would have said, so what—let's do it. But by now I was beginning to realize this wasn't ordinarily.

Bambi had booked me in at the Westminster Hotel,

which is nice and quiet. It was also three blocks from the Ritz, where (naturally) everyone else was staying. That meant I was close enough for meetings and stuff without having to run into my "colleagues" any more than necessary.

As soon as I got to the hotel I threw my suitcase into the room and called Lisa to meet me at Chez Julien. This was my big idea, having read about it in the American Express travel magazine. It seemed like a place Lisa and I would like.

Lisa was already waiting for me inside, wearing this really nice tweed blazer and pale-beige blouse which picked up the gold in her hair and, of course, jeans. I suppose she or I could have made some joke about my being worried about kissing her when I had a cold before, but now we were just happy to see each other. We kissed and kept quiet about it.

Finally, we decided to walk around and look things over. It was practically empty that afternoon, so we could use it like a museum. We checked out the skylight and all the murals, and Lisa filled me in on the Art Nouveau style.

As it turned out a lot of students and artists and other penniless types usually frequent there, so the food was extremely cheap. But I have to say, it wasn't bad. It is Paris, after all. I ordered a salad and *coq au vin* to keep things simple and Lisa had turbot poached in white wine.

Meanwhile, Lisa brought me up to date on the race for the municipal council. She and a couple of other students were conducting a poll on what the people in the district wanted most. It was her idea and Professor Thomer was all for it.

Now as I said, the place was empty, but about halfway through our meal the waiter comes and puts another couple at our table, for his convenience. Anyway, they sat down, an artist and his model, and he started doing sketches of her. They spoke in French, so it was easy for me to ignore them. The next arrival was a wino. An old French stewbum who kind of staggered in and was seated at the table behind Lisa, with his back to her. After him came four teenaged guys. They sat at the next table over and made plenty of noise, fake burps and all that garbage, and threw napkins at each other. Here I wanted to get this big romantic thing going and all of a sudden we're in the middle of a zoo. About this point the wino passed out and his head fell directly on Lisa's back. She laughed and got up and gently arranged him so he could sleep with his head in his arms.

The artist's model turned to us, and with a smile gestured around the place and said in English: "Paradise lost."

We nodded, finished up, and left, walking to the Boulevard de Sebastopol. From there we started toward the river Seine. The sun was out and the air was clear. Lisa was trying to show the city to me, but all I cared about was that I was with her.

However, she was intent on being my guide. We turned onto the Rue de Rivoli, and soon reached the Louvre.

"You said you were interested in art, right?" Lisa reaffirmed when we entered the museum. She was on home territory.

Now I know this is going to sound kind of uncultural, but what I did while she was lecturing was compare practically everything to her. Hell, the artists would have liked that, I think. Like I would check the *Mona Lisa's* smile against my Lisa's. And I had Lisa stand so I could compare the *Venus de Milo's* body to hers. (Lisa won—not that I had any firsthand knowledge of either.) One thing did not generate any comparisons to

Lisa: Géricault's *Raft of the Medusa.* I did decide the big.painting of shipwrecked people clinging to a raft and climbing over one another reminded me of Hollywood. We finished up at the *Winged Victory.* Lisa went up in front of it and stretched her arms out in a victory sign for me. That way I could look at two goddesses at once.

It was dark by the time we got to the Latin Quarter. I guess it was in my head, but I could feel a lot of pressure on me to do something about our sexual relations, which were, as I've said, zilch. It was really funny that I would feel that much consternation over it. I mean, you don't spend time on locations or hanging around shows and studios and not meet lots of lovelies. And let's face it, I'm not bad-looking. I'm not a pretty boy, that's not my quality, but I'm no ugly. I would say I am good-looking without being pretty. Maybe even ruggedly good-looking. That I've heard from casting directors. So given I'm good-looking and she's good-looking (to me, she was beautiful) and we're getting along famously and all that, well, hell, I really didn't want to rush it.

That doesn't mean I didn't want to get there. To sex, that is. It just meant not all at once. At least, that's what I kept telling myself. Maybe what I was really afraid of was getting her mad. Everything was so nice and I liked being with Lisa so much I didn't want to do anything to mess it up. Besides, I'll admit it, I was kind of scared. I mean, what if we did and she was, well, disappointed. I had never had those thoughts before. Hell, there are chicks all over L.A. who can provide sterling references as to my ability to satisfy. But Lisa was special. Different. Important.

These are the kinds of thoughts I was having as we turned off the Boulevard St. Germain onto the Boulevard St. Michel. I also noticed we had picked up some company. There was a guy walking along with us, staring at Lisa and not saying a word.

She told him to shove off in French but he kept right alongside.

"What's with this jag-off?" I asked.

"Who knows? Anyway, he's just trying to annoy us," she said. "Don't pay any attention."

He was walking right with us.

"I don't like the way he's leering at you," I said.

"Really, Michael? You haven't been doing so bad yourself."

"What I do is not leering."

"Oh?"

"Those are adoring glances."

"So who said you could look but not touch?" she said with a smile.

I couldn't let Lisa's remark go unretorted.

"Well, for one thing, Lisa, you haven't stood still long enough for me to try anything. And for another, this son of a bitch has got to go."

Obviously, I am slow to anger. And I am almost never moved to violence. But as the intent of Lisa's words started coming through I figured I had better get rid of Fido so I could have Lisa to myself. I sized him up and he was, if anything, a little bigger than I am.

I stepped in front of the guy and faced him.

There's a look I give that I can only give when I mean it. Namely, my "I-am-ready-to-kill-if-I-have-to" look. I meant it. And it was obviously translating into French, because the guy read me perfectly. He shuffled around a little bit. Then he crossed the street and went back the other way.

Neither Lisa nor I said anything. She took my arm and we walked by the Seine. Soon we crossed a bridge to the Île de la Cité.

She stopped.

"Look up," she said, very quietly.

Behind her, silhouetted by the moon, was the tower of the Cathedral of Notre Dame. The gothic arches seemed to direct my eyes up and up to the top. It was beautiful in the night. After looking up, I was aware Lisa was facing me. I looked at her and she was looking up at me. We kissed a long time.

When we were done we kept standing there in front of Notre Dame. Really, I believed the cathedral was a sanctification of the way we felt.

"Lisa," I began.

She took my hand and whispered to me:

"C'mon, Michael, there's more."

I followed her. I was ready to follow her anywhere.

Lisa led me back to the bridge. Beside it were some steps that took us down to the river. We walked along the bank to a little park. A gigantic Russian wolfhound appeared. He stood on the side of the hill, looking us over in the lamplight. We must have met his approval, because in a very stately way he trotted back up the hill to his master.

We were alone. I wasn't really sure I wanted to be. I was getting petrified of making the wrong move, of breaking the mood, of doing anything that would make Lisa feel I would be false to the moment. We saw a bench and sat down. There was the river in the lamplight. The glow highlighted her hair, too. And in the dark the pupils of her eyes were large and black with halos of green. Lisa put her hand very softly on the back of my neck and we kissed.

Okay, I did do something. I mean, I had to. I put my hand over her breast. Lisa realized I wanted to do that and it was honest. And so, in an incredibly natural and easy way, she unbuttoned her blouse and placed my hand inside her bra. We sat like that. With that sense of each other. To me what was incredible was that this was meaning more than anything else with anyone else could have possibly meant. And in its way it was complete. I'm sure that must have been how Lisa felt then. (We never talked about these things, even later—at least, not in a clinical way—the words available were inadequate to our feelings.) There was nothing about this that made me feel we should be going further. I think that's important to understand. And yet, old Mr. Macho was starting to worry about being ready. The result was I literally jumped when Lisa stood up.

"I've got an idea," she said. Oh-oh. Here it comes. My room or hers? Will I be terrific? She pulled me to my feet and started back toward the steps.

"I know the most incredible place for ice cream," she said.

I grabbed her and hugged her.

"Oh, God, Lisa—I love you." I grinned.

She pulled back so she could look at me.

"Jeese, Michael, were you that hungry?"

The place, Glacier Berthillon, was one bridge away, on the Île St. Louis. And Lisa was right. It was excellent. Especially when you're a coffee-ice-cream freak. I have had coffee ice cream all over the world (I also recommend the coffee cooler at the Old World restaurant on Sunset Boulevard in Los Angeles) and definitely this went right off the rating charts.

Lisa decided to put things back in their proper perspective.

"Well, Mike, if you're through licking the sides of the dish, I'm ready for bed," she said, leaning forward.

Well fed (I had also included some of their cassis sorbet) and with renewed confidence, I was not one to back away from a challenge.

"So all it takes is ice cream?" I asked, rubbing my hands.

"No-no-no, I'm really ready for *bed* bed," she clarified. "I've got an early seminar."

Actually, I had a rehearsal thing in the morning myself. Besides, Lisa didn't leave any room for dispute. I finished off the last two drops of ice cream and both our wafers. We went out to the street.

"Listen, it's too late to mess around with the Métro, Lisa. Let me get you a cab."

"Okay."

"You're so easy," I said, waving one over. When the car pulled up, I gave Lisa money for the fare. I sure had the cash and I knew she was counting pennies. But when we kissed goodnight she slipped the money back in my pocket.

"Let's do this again sometime," Lisa said, jumping in the taxi.

I stood there long after it had pulled away.

Chapter

6

IT was one of those rare times O'Connor and I were at odds. First, because of the movie. And second, because of my being tied up with Lisa.

The thing on the film was this: Wesley wanted to wrap on schedule after Paris; I wanted to go back to Scotland and do the scenes he took out when I got sick. Naturally, since O'Connor was the producer he didn't want to go over budget, so he was down on the Scottish reshoot. Well, tough! I was going to the wall on this one. Fact was, I had really put my neck out, challenging the director. But I was the guy people were going to see on the screen. No fucking way was I giving up without a battle.

So I called Eve.

Now this, boys and girls, was the time to see if Eve was worth her percentage. She struck like lightning. She convinced Ron Peters to get on a plane with her to Paris. Ultimately, it was his movie. He was going to have to decide if the thing went into editorial right then, or back to Scotland to pick up my shots. It would be a real showdown.

In point of fact, Ron's coming over made O'Connor blissfully happy; he was off the hook on making the decision. O'Connor decided to celebrate by going out and looking for women (actually, he'd do that to celebrate having eggs for breakfast), and he asked me to go along. This was when Lisa was finally explained to him. I told him I was playing it straight.

O'Connor couldn't believe his ears.

"You're not coming with me to Pig Alley?" he gasped. Note: He insisted on pronouncing Pigalle as Pig Alley—an extinct Second World War gag.

"You heard me, Bob."

O'Connor was standing in the middle of his room at the Ritz, holding his five-o'clock double bourbon, and deciding between his polyester wine blazer or his double-knit blue sport jacket with the red piping.

"You got something, boy," Bob said, "and you got it bad."

Understand, I really have to stick up for O'Connor. When we were on a picture together, he often was all that got me through some pretty draggy times. I liked the guy. And besides, it was an unwritten rule between us not to get so hooked with some chick as to be unavailable for a little "tomcattin'," as he put it. Well, here I was, really stiffing the guy and going off on my own. But let's face it, I wasn't into what he wanted to do, and besides, I had a real commitment to Lisa. Not that I expected him to understand. I mean, he hadn't even met Lisa. All he knew was I was seeing a lady. And obviously, by the way I was acting, she was a lot different from the general run of chickies that kept my old friend going.

Ah, but go he did. Bob told me he lived by one credo: "I never waste time fighting temptation." Even though we had known each other in L.A. it wasn't until we were on a picture in Hong Kong that I had the chance—no, the honor and privilege—to see Bob in action. It was O'Connor who discovered the kindly Dr. Wang, who allowed Bob to order one from column A and one from column B. Yes, he really was ready to go again in a half-hour.

A few weeks ago in Casablanca he had hardly missed me, though. He met the local holder of the Dr. Wang franchise: Raschid. Personally, I don't know how he got out alive. I'm convinced the Bob O'Connors of this world have special angels.

"Okay, Michael, what's the name of this new piece of quiff?"

"Listen, moron, her name is Lisa."

That wasn't the end of it for Bob.

"So tell me, Mike baby, how's her snatch?"

"It's not that kind of relationship."

"Sure, you're letting ol' Bob lone-wolf it just so you can hold hands in private."

"Think what you want, you big jag-off."

"Touch-y. As I recall you were the original member of the beaver patrol, right, boy?"

"I told you this is different."

He really took off on that.

"What? Different? You mean she doesn't have one? You're so full of shit. You're talking to buddy Bob, remember, and I know you'd jump a snake if it'd hold still long enough. C'mon, Mike baby, we'll go get ourselves a couple of dollies and a quart of Wesson oil."

"No way, pal," I said. "Besides, I'm meeting Lisa now at the Sorbonne."

"Oh, an intellectual. I know, it must be a mind fuck."

Bob convulsed in laughter as I threw ice cubes from his drink at him.

"All right, Mike, all right," he howled. "It's wuv, sweet wuv. So bring her around."

"She was at the location," I said.

"You couldn't have been very proud of her if you didn't introduce her."

"I just didn't want her to find out what scumbags my friends are."

Bob splashed Canoe all over himself.

"All right," he said, opening the door, "let's you and I go work the lobby—for old times' sake."

"Not now."

He put his hand on my shoulder as we headed out.

"Wait a minute, Mike. Did you say her name was Lisa?"

"Yeah."

"Lisa what?"

"Lisa none of your beeswax."

"No, really."

"Lisa Foster."

"Oh, yeah, Lisa Foster."

"C'mon, O'Connor, you never heard of her."

"Sure I have . . . screws like a mink in heat."

He screamed appropriately when I booted him in the ass.

My meeting place with Lisa was not your standard out-of-the-way rendezvous. She had asked me to come to class with her. Well, actually, she had told me where her class was and invited me to show up. Seeing as how I wanted to see Lisa, I showed.

It was not all that easy to find the room. And I've also got to tell you I was a little edgy about how the students would take my being an American. Okay, I know that sounds paranoid, but I remembered they had all those riots at the Sorbonne. Besides, I've never seen anyone on the TV news from Europe demonstrating *for* the U.S.

Anyway, I got to the class, and nobody gave a shit what I was. It occurred to me I might catch a glimpse of Philippe Budin, but he was long gone from his brief scene. The class was in a lecture hall. I spotted Lisa, who was standing right up near the front of the room. She was wearing this great Scandinavian turtleneck sweater and carrying on an argument (later she insisted to me it was a debate—on Marat's role in the French revolution) and tying it into the current election, and the whole thing was in French. Even though I wasn't able to understand a word, I decided she made a lot of sense. I couldn't have been too far off, because the class seemed to be with her.

"I don't know what you said," I told Lisa while the class emptied, "but I agree with every word."

"Great, but you're not the teacher."

"I'll bet I can teach you a few things."

"I never study in bed," she whispered.

She introduced me to the prof whose campaign she was working on: Professor Thomer. He was a nice old guy with a white mustache and goatee who raved about Lisa and said she was really making a difference. After that, we went out to the street. The weather was brisk, but it didn't bother us. One of the guys from her class came up and they spoke in French for a few minutes before he left.

"I must have done pretty good," Lisa congratulated herself. "He says I've got both the communists and the Gaullists mad at me."

"Really?" I said, at her announced accomplishment.

"Well, not mad—but thinking, anyway."

"Now that's the mark of a real politician," I decided. "You could be the one running for office."

"I don't know about that, Michael, but I do think I can help out the government in Canada."

"If it's like ours, they need all the help they can get,"
I said, showing my political savvy.

"I'm thinking with the French separatist movement
in Quebec, English-speaking Canada is going to need
people who can work with Quebec and France."

My brilliant analytical mind was hard at work.

"Which is why you're studying here," I deduced.

"I'm afraid it is."

I was a little bewildered.

"You got a problem?"

"The problem, sweet Michael, is that my best chance
for a political career is in Canada," she told me with
unassailable logic.

"I figured you wouldn't go far in Topeka."

"Or in Paris."

Eureka!

"You really like it here, don't you, Lisa?"

"I'm beginning to, you turkey," she said, ruffling my
hair.

It crossed my mind I had plans for her in Los Angeles,
but I didn't want to get into that. I mean, it was only a
possibility, but it was a possibility that was getting
stronger all the time. In the meantime, what could she
do in Paris?

"Maybe you can find something here?" I asked.

"Yeah, you got any movie deals for me?" she kidded.

We walked on while I thought that over seriously.
Maybe Ron Peters knew somebody in the studio's Paris
office.

"As a matter of fact, Ron Peters, our executive producer, is coming in for a meeting. What if . . . " I began.

I stopped. Lisa stood waiting for me to lay the big
idea on her. Little did she know this was all a plot to
finesse her into the movie business. Then she'd have a
reason to come to L.A., right?

"Hey, Lisa, I'll take you to the meeting and introduce

you and maybe something'll come of it, you know, for the Paris office."

She wasn't exactly jumping up and down.

"I don't know, Michael," she said.

"No, it's perfect," I said. "You can meet Eve, too."

"Eve?"

"Sure, everybody's wanting to meet you," I bubbled. "O'Connor and Bambi—"

"Eve? Your agent?"

I looked at Lisa. The eyes were wide and her face was showing a kind of abject fear.

"Hey, Eve isn't that bad." I thought a moment, then modified that. "Well, really she is, but she's got to meet you."

At the very least I figured this would let Eve know who I've been keeping company with. That should get her off my ass about hitting on some French actress types. Meanwhile, Lisa was trying real hard to get through to me.

"I don't think you understand, Michael. Those people do not want to meet me."

"Why? You're terrific, you're pretty, you speak two languages, you come from a beautiful part of the world—"

She started walking away. Without thinking I grabbed her arm.

"Hey, I'm talking to you."

She looked down at my hand on her arm. I removed it.

"Michael, don't give me that hype, okay?" she said. "If you want to impress me, I can see that, but don't hand me a line of crapola about them wanting to meet me."

And then she added, "I'm nobody."

We stood there on the street.

"You're somebody to me, Lisa, and I want them to know it."

She just shook her head, saying nothing for a moment.

"I don't think you realize how different we are," she said finally.

"Vive la différence," I said, making curvy outlines with my hands.

She was having none of it.

"C'mon, Michael, don't you know this is all a colossal accident?" she asked, without waiting for an answer. "You should be with someone who fits in, who goes with all that money and glamour." She was practically pleading. "Not me, not Miss Nobody. I don't belong—not with them and not with you—"

"Cut it out, Lisa."

"Yeah, Lisa, Lisa Nobody from Constance Falls, Ontario."

"Please."

"Listen. So we have fun for a while. Then . . ."

She sighed. People were passing by us. I lowered my voice, even though it was unlikely anyone could understand.

"My friend, Bob O'Connor, said he wanted to meet you."

"He doesn't know me from diddly-squat."

"Listen, I don't keep you a secret, do you understand?" I was getting a little perturbed.

"Oh."

"And furthermore, as far as my saying you're pretty and smart and all, that happens to be what I believe, for Christ's sake."

She didn't even say "oh" to that.

"And besides," I continued, "I can't believe you're such a big chicken."

She brushed a few strands of gold hair from her forehead and looked around.

"These are real Hollywood film people, huh?"

"Sure."

She took my hand and put it back on her arm where I had it before.

"You know, you could turn out to be a nice guy after all. Maybe it would be kind of interesting."

We started walking along again.

"Anyway, Lisa, O'Connor invited us to meet him in Pigalle this evening."

"It's kind of a tacky place," she said, "but fun."

She had no sooner said that than I stopped a cab.

The Place Pigalle was loaded with lights and people. We were sure O'Connor would come staggering out of the Moulin Rouge or the Folies Bergère (we did go in and check out the can-can), but no luck.

Lisa would just have to meet the whole crew all at once.

Chapter

7

RON Peters decreed the meeting would be held in his suite at the Hôtel Plaza-Athénée. So what? It was no surprise everyone would have to go over to him. (Everyone, that is, but Eve; she always stayed at the Plaza-Athénée.) It was a way of showing who was the boss. Whatever, I wasn't going to get pissed off at Ron, too—I had enough problems with Wesley. Besides, today was the *big day*. We would see whether I counted for anything in this picture. It wasn't as if I was some big important star, but I really felt we didn't have what we needed on film. I had to push for it. Anyway, what's the worst thing that could happen? So I'd be back doing bit parts and looking for another break. Well, maybe I was a little nervous.

"You want to fill me in on what's going on?" Lisa asked. She had put aside the student look for the occasion. Under her trench coat Lisa wore this terrific tailored maroon blouse, a pleated gray skirt, and, get this, heels. Sitting beside her in the cab gave me a good chance to study her legs. I prayed for traffic while I answered her question.

"When I got sick in Scotland," I reminded her, "the director went ahead and did a lot of stuff without me."

"So?"

"So I want him to do it over with me in it."

"I don't understand why your agent and the boss have to come," she said. "Sounds like somebody just wants a trip to Paris."

"Lisa, I assure you those people can come to Paris whenever they please; they don't need an excuse."

There was plenty of traffic. I was getting worried about being late.

"But that doesn't explain why there's this big meeting," she insisted.

"Because Wesley's the director and he says the film is fine just the way it is."

"If he's the director, why are you arguing with him?" she asked. It was a question Wesley would have seconded.

"Because he's wrong."

"And I thought trying to get somebody elected was complicated. Why is your agent here?"

"She's supposed to look out for my interests in this, but I doubt it."

Lisa cocked her head slightly on that.

"Do I have to be nice to these assholes?"

"They are not just assholes, Lisa. They are also talented people."

"You're a talented people, too."

"Maybe that's why none of us get along."

I wasn't sure if I had answered all her questions. The truth was, there really would be a lot going on at this meeting. For one thing, it could amount to the end of my whole goddam career. I mean, I really had no business to challenge Wesley. As I'd told Lisa, he was the director.

What was really a dumb-ass move on my part was to

drag Lisa along to this meeting. Number one, instead of a nice fun social thing, she was going to see a big blowup about all kinds of shit that wouldn't mean anything to her. And number two, if this all went against me I would get my nuts cut off today.

Besides, I really didn't give two shits if she met them or vice-versa. It was just I wanted Lisa to know the kind of crap I have to put up with. Also, Eve should know what was going on in my life.

"I think that's the hotel there," Lisa said, pointing. "Jesus! It looks like a parking lot for limousines!"

The front of the Plaza-Athénée was lined with Rolls-Royces and Bentleys and Daimlers. And I thought the Ritz was a big deal (if they let Wesley Crouch and Bob O'Connor in there, how big a deal could it be?), but this was, well, opulent. I remembered productions where I stayed at people's apartments.

"Look!" Lisa exclaimed.

I missed it, but Lisa was certain she'd seen Audrey Hepburn get into one of the limos and be driven away. I told her it was possible and she was even more likely to run into Orson Welles or Jackie Onassis at this hotel. With that, I figured this would put my place in filmdom in proper perspective for Lisa. And then again, I reminded myself, the movie wasn't out yet, either.

"Are you sure I should be coming to this meeting?" Lisa inquired, for the ten billionth time.

"I asked you, didn't I?" I answered, in a display of rhetorical nonsense.

"No way do I belong here, Michael."

Obviously, Lisa was again expressing a highly developed sense of her place in society. Probably something inbred from Canada's British heritage, and all that pip-pip-old-chap class-structure bullshit. On top of that, she was a student, with all the social awareness commensurate with the occupation.

"To think you guys are spending all this money just to have a meeting," she said.

"It's in the executive producer's hotel room, Lisa," I explained, apologetically. "He's got to sleep somewhere."

"There are people in India paying rent to sleep on sidewalks," she said, as the doorman came up to our taxi.

We got out and went inside. Lisa gasped as she looked around the lobby under the big dome. It was gold and turquoise and, how can I put it—rich. Ultra-rich. No one in particular was near us, but Lisa felt compelled to whisper.

"Michael, I'll bet I'm the first person from Constance Falls ever to walk in here."

She took my arm and we went up to Ron's room.

If the lobby was Paris class, inside Ron Peter's room was pure Hollywood trash. Wesley was wearing leather pants and a Qiana shirt open to the third button, and had plenty of gold and turquoise showing. What a turd. He must have been color-keyed to the lobby. Bambi was scurrying around, putting out pencils and yellow legal pads for notes. There were also three lanky gals draped around the room. One was oriental, one was black, and one was Swedish.

"Hey, Mike baby, what'd you bring to the party?"

It was O'Connor. He threw a bear hug around Lisa and gave her a big smooch on the cheek. She looked at me helplessly. I echoed her sentiments. The whole thing was embarrassing hell out of me, but I was stuck now. She let me help her off with her coat. I had to stay—it was my meeting.

"Where'd you get the furniture?" I asked, motioning to the girls.

"Rent-a-floozie," Bob replied.

He released Lisa long enough for me to make a slightly more formal introduction. Immediately Bob took her by the hand and walked up to Wesley.

"This is the director, Wesley Crouch," O'Connor said, like an impresario. "Wesley, meet Lisa Foster—dynamite chick."

Wesley raised his glasses to his forehead in recognition and smiled. Lisa smiled back.

Bambi came by on her way to check something. (Bambi was always checking on something.) She nodded to the exchange of names and kept right on going. More time was available with the three girls: Toshiko, Claudette, and Birgitta. Lisa began a conversation with them in French, but it didn't seem to last long. Bob and Bambi got busy setting up an easel to display some photographs of the filming. There seemed to be an aura of anticipatory activity, even though in fact nothing was happening. All of this, I was so painfully aware with Lisa watching, was our little island of tinsel. It was set dressing for Ron, who was still in the bedroom. No question, Ron Peters was getting his money's worth of bullshit.

Meanwhile, no Eve in sight. Although Bambi told us five times Eve had called from her room to say she was on her way.

In the midst of this, I felt Lisa tapping me on the shoulder.

"Can I ask you a little favor?" she whispered. (Suddenly, she seemed to be suffering from loss of voice.)

"Sure," I said jauntily. "What would you like?"

"I would like to get the hell out of here."

"So would I, Lisa."

"Yeah, but they pay you for this, Mr. Hollywood," she said. "I'm only here as a tourist."

"C'mon, you haven't even met Eve yet."

"Good, that means there's still time," she said hopefully.

I tried to keep her busy by taking her over to look at

the production stills on the easel. There were pictures of Wesley talking to the cameraman, Wesley studying the landscape, Wesley laughing, Wesley reading the script (a faked shot if I ever saw one), and Wesley talking to Bob and Bambi.

"Jeeso-peeso," she said, "it looks like Wesley does everything—where are you?"

"In the film," I snarled.

The documentation of paranoia in actors is well known throughout the recorded history of the theater. That aside, it was with great pleasure I was able to show Lisa that the egomania of directors gives a lot of credence to any actor's particular anxieties. But Jesus H. Christ! Why is it I thought I had to prove my case? Lisa didn't doubt me anyway. She took a larger view of things than that.

"Michael, now I'm beginning to see why all you people are nuts."

I had rather hoped she would exclude me from her diagnosis.

"You see," she went on, "you're all thinking you're the one person responsible for the picture, and you know it takes a group to do it."

"I guess you're right," I said. Hell, guess? She *was* right.

"But then, in another way, you alone can be responsible for whether it's good or crap."

"You just figured out the movies," I complimented her.

She smiled up at me.

"Okay, but I'd really rather clear brush in Ontario," she said. She squeezed my hand harder than ever and added, "Or spend a night with you."

That caught me for a moment. I was working on a comeback when Lisa walked up to Wesley.

"Mr. Crouch?" she asked. "In *Sierra Sun* did you

intend to portray the leader of the Mexican guerrillas as a symbol of Christ?"

Wesley turned in his chair. My stomach turned in my body. Where the hell did she find out about that film? I mean, just because it is the one that made his career, it still has a lot of technical flaws.

"As a matter of fact"—Wesley was beaming—"I did just that, over the objections of the producer."

He blabbed on another fifteen minutes about the film, and the battles it took to produce.

I dragged Lisa aside.

"Where did you find out about that film?" I hissed.

"Did you forget I'm a student?" she whispered. "I saw it at a university film festival."

"Actually, I think I saw it too, on late-night television," I said. "It wasn't that great."

"Well, yesterday I looked up some of the current criticism about it. Your feelings are in the minority."

I was wondering whether Lisa had looked up anything about me (she hadn't, so I mentioned the dates on my *New West* magazine reviews) when Eve made her entrance.

"Wesley, Bob—have I held things up for long?" Eve asked, sweeping into the room.

"No," O'Connor replied, motioning to the bedroom. "Ron's still on the phone."

Eve, looking slightly disappointed, sat down just to the right of the head of the table.

"Hi, Eve," I said.

Eve reached out her hand to me and I shook it. She pulled me to her and offered her cheek for me to kiss, something we never do in private.

"Let me handle this, understand?" she ordered out of the side of her mouth.

"That's why you're here, Eve," I said.

I straightened up and brought Lisa beside me. It

struck me how terrific Lisa looked in this room. She was standing with her hands in the pockets of her skirt, tastefully dressed and not the least bit showy.

"Eve, this is my friend, Lisa Foster."

I wondered why the hell I introduced her as my friend. To signify we had some relationship? Or to put Eve off the real course?

Lisa nodded. Her hands came out of her pockets. Eve looked at her. Neither spoke. Was it a standoff? Finally, Lisa came up with a "Michael's told me a lot about you."

Gotcha! Lisa had to speak first. Hollywood bitch—1. Young pretty student—0.

"Come now," Eve responded, "you two can't be that hard up for conversation."

Lisa smiled. I could tell she was fascinated. Eve, though small, just sat there and emanated power. (Lisa told me later she had never seen anyone in such control of a situation as Eve Ross.)

Eve waved to Bambi.

"Bambi, be a dear and check if Robert Evans is staying here at the hotel," she said breezily.

Eve got back to me and business, as usual.

"Michael, did you see any dailies?"

"Not of Scotland," said the wronged star.

My agent looked a little bewildered. I explained I had gone over the script, so I knew what was supposed to have been in the picture. Then there was the matter of Wesley's feelings toward me, or rather against me. I gave a look to Lisa on this point; she looked back, knowingly. There were also Wesley's views toward star roles in general, and his whole move to shift away from building up my part.

Eve listened to all of this, got up and walked us to where no one else could hear, and commented:

"All that horseshit aside, Michael, you feel you're not there enough in the Scottish sequence."

Why did I bring Lisa to this?

"What I said is not exactly horseshit, Eve."

Eve addressed Lisa.

"What do you do when Mike's not annoying you?"

"I study political science," Lisa answered.

"At the Sorbonne," I added, just in case Eve had ever heard of it.

"Political science?" Eve repeated.

That's right, Eve baby, there's something out there that's not the title for a new TV series or the name of some in restaurant.

"Well, then," Eve went on, "if you're interested in politics this meeting won't be a total waste of time for you."

"Oh, no," Lisa agreed. She said that so sweetly I really think she meant: Yes, it will be a waste of time—but not a total waste.

Eve checked again to make sure Wesley was out of range and commenced to explain how even if we forced Wesley to shoot the scenes (which meant a move back to Scotland) he could still cut them out of the movie. *However*—she interrupted herself to ask us what time it was in Los Angeles, then had me bring her a phone so she could make an overseas call—the studio had final cut. *Therefore* (she addressed herself to Lisa to impress her, which she did) the plan was to make sure Ron ordered Wesley to do the reshoot. *Then* Wesley would know Michael had to be in the final picture as much as or more than intended.

"You could be President," Lisa said, obviously impressed more than was actually warranted by Eve's plan.

"Smart girl you have here, Michael," Eve said.

"That's why we're friends," I said. Jesus, there's that friends thing again.

Lisa gave me a kind of "how am I doing?" look. I returned a kind of a "little too well" squint.

Eve started to make another call when the door to the bedroom opened. We beheld Ron Peters, dressed for business in a blue suit and tie. He came to the head of the table and sat down. Eve quickly sat next to him.

"Okay, let's get started," Ron said, knowing full well he was the only reason we had not begun.

Ron Peters had started in film sales, working with the theater owners—the exhibitors. He moved up through the distributor ranks to a studio executive position. After that, he went on his own to form his own company. He had coproduced his first film a few years before; it was a success. So were the next two. Then came three failures in a row, followed by a real profit maker. He was hot again, a forty-nine-year-old *Wunderkind*, and he desperately wanted this picture to make it. Will it be a hit? Or a miss?

Time was tight (time was always tight with Ron Peters), so I did not feel it was necessary to introduce Lisa when Ron shook my hand. She had already sat down anyway, on a couch next to the window.

Bambi got up from the desk and started to take her place at the table.

"Bambi," Ron said, "make sure you check on that call to Burt Lancaster."

She went back to the phone.

O'Connor began going over some budget sheets with Ron. Eve got up and carried her phone over by Lisa on the couch.

"Are you also a student of film?" asked Eve.

"In a way," Lisa replied. Noticing I was listening, she gave an aside to me: "I'm interested in an actor."

"I heard that," Eve said, laughing, and started putting her call through.

Lisa and I also laughed. Briefly. I realized I was a wreck already and the meeting hadn't even started.

"Eve, are you a part of this deal?" Ron asked from the table.

"Absolutely," she answered.

"Well, sit over here where you can hear what we say about you," Ron advised her.

Eve handed the phone to Lisa.

"Honey, when they answer, just say I called and I'll get back to them about four their time."

"Lisa does not work for this production," I said.

"I'd be happy to, Miss Ross," Lisa said, taking the phone as if she had nothing better to do. (She didn't, but that's beside the point.)

"Thanks, and call me Eve," my agent said.

"Yeah, first names," I snorted. "Makes it seem like we're all buddies."

Eve sat down to Ron's right. I was beside her, and Wesley and Bob sat across from us. Bambi sat at the foot of the table, taking notes. The three girls lounged about the room, appropriately.

O'Connor opened hesitantly.

"The thing is, Ron, that Michael feels—"

Ron cut him off.

"Why should I spend another hundred thousand dollars to get a few closeups?" he asked.

Ron does get right to the basic problem. It seemed up to me to express my point of view.

"Well, Ron," I started, "it's—"

"What Michael means, Ron," chimed in my agent, interrupting what I hadn't even begun to say, "is it's a lot more complicated than that."

"Hell, there's nothing complicated at all," Wesley Crouch said, gesturing at us with the glasses which hung by a chain around his neck. "I'm the director and I say we got it."

I held a pad of yellow paper in front of my face, looked over to Lisa, and puffed out my cheeks and rolled up my eyes. Eve kicked my ankle under the table.

"What do you think, Bob?" Ron asked, oblivious about cutting him off before.

"Well, Wesley is the director," Bob said, illuminating the issue with his originality of thought, "but Michael has every right to be concerned because he is the star of the picture."

Bless Bob! May a thousand lovelies descend on his groin!

"That's just it," Eve interjected. "Without those scenes there is not enough coverage of Michael to develop a whole critical part of the picture."

"It couldn't be that bad," Ron said.

"It is if the picture doesn't hold the action," Eve answered, "and doesn't pull the sixteen-to-twenty-fours, much less the twenty-fives and up."

I glanced at Lisa. Obviously she had figured out what that meant. She looked very impressed. For Christ's sake! What the hell did age groups have to do with it? We weren't here to talk demographics. This was an aesthetic question. I wasn't going to put up with this.

"This picture is intended to say something about man and adventure; it's not just a series of goddam explosions!" I blurted.

Eve gave me a dirty look.

"Where is the script?" Ron requested.

"The script is merely a blueprint," Wesley growled. "I'm the one who has to make a picture out of it."

"Where is the script?" Ron repeated.

"Bambi, can we have a script?" Bob delegated the request, and went on, "Ron, you realize that Wesley has gone beyond the script in creating the picture and—"

Ron just looked at Bob and he stopped speaking.

"Here, Ron," Bambi said, walking the script to him.
- Ron looked it over. The writers had been left in L.A.

"What the hell does the script have to do with it?"
Wesley shouted. "Besides, you're talking about editing—
I'll find a way to do that!"

"Your way sucks, Wes," I shouted back. "It's me
who's up there on the goddamn screen."

No one said a word. Eve was mortified. I really had
gone too far. Maybe.

"Do you like living in Paris?" the Swedish girl,
Birgitta, said to Lisa. Everyone turned.

Thank God Lisa didn't answer. O'Connor gave the
girl a shush.

"Oh," Birgitta said, and smiling vapidly, added,
"Sorry."

Lisa didn't even blink through all of this. We turned
back to the table.

"I hate to see all this tension on the set," Ron said,
"but that's got nothing to do with what the picture
looks like."

"Yeah, I remember—" Bob began.

"The way I look at it," Ron continued, "the director's
responsible for the finished film. We're already over
budget. And we are talking about a hundred thousand
more dollars."

I began to sink into deep depression. Wesley was
going to get his way. Son of a bitch!

Eve was not so quick to give up.

"Ron, I know Wesley is concerned about the extra
money," she said, "but think of it as an insurance
premium to give Wesley, and you, all the options you
need for the picture you want."

I never said Eve was dumb. Vindictive, scheming,
cruel, yes. But she's no dummy. She had just given

Wesley a chance to save face. And Ron a warning about the picture.

"That's bullshit!" Wesley said. "I don't need her options."

Ron looked at Bambi.

"Bambi, how long will it take to set up a screening of the dailies from Scotland?"

"I'll call now and find out," Bambi responded.

"I have to make a couple of calls myself," Eve Ross said, heading for the other phone.

After lunch, where we spotted Jean-Paul Belmondo, and during which Eve expressed more curiosity in Lisa than I expected—she asked all about her background, where she was from, her parents (I found out Lisa's dad had been English Canadian, her mother French Canadian)—we all headed over to the screening room. Eve rode with Ron in his chauffeured Rolls, and the rest of us shared cabs.

The way it was working out was probably best, I told myself. We'll look at the film and Ron can make his decision.

"No reserved seats," Bob joked.

Actually, we all took separate seats around the little theater. Lisa sat in the back corner by the projection booth (I had insisted she see this out to the bitter end), and I sat in the middle.

The receptionist came in and told Ron he had a phone call.

"Rack up the film and I'll be back in a minute," Ron said.

When Ron left, Wesley, who was in the front row—although the place was so small none of us were far apart—turned around to talk to me.

"You really think it makes that much difference, Michael?" he asked.

"Absolutely," Eve answered.

"Hell, I don't even know any more," I said.

"Neither do I," Wesley said.

Lisa smiled. I avoided looking at Eve. No one spoke again until Ron came in and sat down.

"Eve," Ron announced, "it looks like a go on that project we discussed."

"I've got a great suggestion for the male lead," she said, smiling at me.

I looked at Lisa. She was beaming. Christ! Doesn't Eve know to double-check with me before she gets me involved in anything?

"Roll 'em," O'Connor yelled.

Bambi picked up the intercom and had the projectionist begin.

We sat and watched the dailies.

There was some film of me at the beginning. It was the first time Lisa had actually seen me on the screen, but if she was impressed she wasn't showing it. Nothing was edited, so there was a lot of the same stuff, over and over. Pretty soon we were into the filler material. Boy, it was taking a long time to get through this. It was what I had expected, Wesley didn't have enough. Oh hell, I wasn't the editor, could I be sure? Ron probably wouldn't agree with me. Why didn't I keep my big mouth shut? What was Lisa going to think?

The lights went on.

Ron looked around the room for final opinions.

"Wes?" he asked.

"I can make it with what's there."

"Bob?"

"I can see it works, and then maybe it doesn't, but it's really not fair to see this without all the stuff from

Casablanca and Tangiers, of course, it should stand by itself, but . . ."

"Eve?"

"Ron, I think it's really up to you now," she said.

Of course, Eve would say something patronizing like that. I mean, she's already worrying about her next deal with Ron Peters.

"I wondered when somebody would realize that," Ron said, getting up. He looked at O'Connor and Wesley and told them, "Finish up here in a week. I'll go back to Scotland with you to pick up the new footage."

He looked around to see if there was any argument. There was none.

"And then we'll get our butts back to L.A.," he commanded.

Somehow I didn't feel like cheering. Wesley suggested to me we should get together on what I had in mind. I met Lisa when she came out of her aisle. Now she knew what an underhanded cutthroat business this all was. I mean, the way Eve had manipulated the whole situation to her advantage.

Lisa and I reached the door the same time as Eve.

"Well, Lisa, you sure got the whole show today," Eve said.

"I can see why Michael thinks you're the best," Lisa said.

"I do?" I said, with real surprise. "Oh, yes, I do."

Eve smiled and walked out ahead of us. We followed slowly, dropping back from the rest.

Lisa looked up at me.

"You know the most important thing I heard today?" she asked me.

I gave her a blank look. What? The new project? The reshoot?

"That Ron said you've got another week in Paris."

Chapter

8

LIKE just about everything else with Lisa our first experience of sex happened without planning. In a way, I think it just kind of overtook us.

Not that I want to make too big a deal out of it. I mean, I see now I was gone over her on a kiss. Everything else, and it took a hell of a long time to get to everything else, was only the natural outcome of two people caring about each other. And in our case, as we'd never cared about anyone else before—or ever could again.

All we had in mind was to spend the next few (and what were supposed to be my last) days in Paris together. The idea of going away from Lisa was making me feel pretty crappy. I think, though, we just decided to ignore that (hah!) and try to have a good time.

What that meant really was trying to be together as much as possible.

"Okay, how long am I'm supposed to sit around down here?"

It was Lisa calling up from the lobby at the Westminster. She was waiting? She must have thought I would meet her downstairs. I guess I really should have gone over to her place—something I had yet to do—but I had to do travel arranging today. Bambi had already left for Glasgow to get things set up, so I was supposed to take care of my own tickets to Scotland, and the Air France office was near the hotel. I went down to the lobby. Lisa looked amazing. She had on this green sweater and a Black Watch plaid skirt, and these dark-green knee socks. Definitely worth staying over for.

We walked out into the bright and fashionable Paris morning. This was to be, I decided, a perfect day. Just walking around, together. We walked along holding hands to the Air France office. As it was, the day practically came to a halt there. I mean, I really learned how much I appreciated what Bambi did. Even Lisa speaking French didn't help—they were slow in any language.

So we sat.

"At least, Michael, we're spending the day together. Even if it is sitting."

"Yeah, I can't believe I'm going through all this trouble when I don't even want to leave!"

Finally, they came back and told us the tickets wouldn't be ready for another couple of hours.

We decided there wasn't much sense in going too far away, so we kind of wandered out looking for something to do. Lisa took me past the Opéra to the Rue Lafayette. There (ta-da!) she introduced me to the Galeries Lafayette, the biggest department store in Paris.

Now I've got to tell you, I can really get into a department store. I mean, I treat them like museums. It's educational. And here was all that fantastic stuff—

en français—which really tells you where the people are. Or wish they were.

Not that we were on a shopping trip. Just looking. And the main attraction for me was Lisa. Lisa under that great huge dome of the main building, or Lisa trying on wigs and hats. And, oh yes, the toys. I still can't believe they didn't kick us out. Particularly when we put on plastic knight helmets and got in a fight with plastic swords. The toy department was also where the dolls were. Beautiful lacy French dolls, dressed in eighteenth-century style. Maybe it was the temptation of all that merchandise that led Lisa to break one of her long-standing rules: "Thou shalt not let Michael buy thee any presents." What she picked—well, really fell in love with—was a ridiculous little stuffed lion. Not the fancy Steiff kind, mind you, just a little inexpensive kind of cute lion. She named it, wouldn't you know, Mikey. I paid for it and crudely asked if she wanted anything else. Of course not, it was just Mikey had to come from me. And that was all she wanted. She wouldn't budge on that point. I wanted to buy her so much more.

Next stop was the restaurant in the Galeries Lafayette. It was snack time for the three of us. Mikey refused to eat, but I had no trouble scarfing down some chicken. About halfway through, I noticed a poster of Chartres Cathedral.

"Now there's a place I've never been—Chartres," I said, as if I had been everywhere else.

Lisa was kind enough to overlook my temporary lapse into pomposity.

"Just one more thing we have in common," she said, trying to get Mikey to take a little pastry.

"You've never been to Chartres either?" I asked.

"No," replied Lisa.

I had a brainstorm.

"Wanna go?"

"To Chartres?"

"Earth to Lisa, earth to Lisa," I broadcast, chiding her for not keeping up, "we are talking about Chartres, right?"

"But it's out in the country."

"So I'll rent a car." I had all the answers.

"When?"

"Now."

Lisa had one more caveat.

"What if the weather gets bad?" she asked.

"We can worry about that when we get there," I said smugly.

"There's a rally tonight where Thomer is speaking."

"I thought you weren't going anyway."

Lisa didn't say anything else. Oh. What about sleeping arrangements? Was that holding her up?

"Of course, I'll find out about rooms before we go," I promised.

Lisa looked at the poster.

"Don't call ahead," she said. "That way I'll have something else to worry about besides the weather."

Okay, so you can say we both knew what was possible. But really I think we just weren't dealing with it right then.

There's a Hertz rental right in the store. Actually, it's in the second building of the store. A very simple matter. What was complicated was we would have to go to their Porte de St.-Cloud office to pick it up. Now came the logistics. Lisa and I both had to get some overnight stuff, and I had to get my ticket. We decided to split up and meet back at Air France.

When she finally came walking in (I was sure she'd

back out) I had already been there forty-five minutes
getting my ticket. I mean, the idea was to get away and
enjoy ourselves. Although I had no idea what we were
getting away from. Hell, I was exhausted from all the
arrangements. But seeing Lisa with her bag over her
shoulder perked me right up.

By the time we picked up the car and got on the road
it was already dark. And raining. And I had never been
in a Renault 16 before.

"Why aren't there any wipers on this heap?"

"Try this, Michael."

"That's the horn, Lisa."

"No kidding, Michael—I figured that honking meant
something. How about this button thing?"

"Lisa, you wanna turn the lights back on?"

We did get the wipers to work, but it was no go on the
heater. For that we gave up and stopped at a gas
station on the highway. Can you believe I had to get a
mechanic to show us how to turn on the heater? He
wished me *Bon chance*—good luck. Thanks, fella.

Without the rain, it would have been an easy drive.
The village of Chartres was practically a suburb. (Not
that we could get a look at it in the dark.) We drove
around the narrow eleventh-century streets looking for
a place to stay. There were a couple of false stops. At
last we found our home at Le Boeuf Couronné inn and
restaurant. I considered this excellent, because I really
did not want to go back out and drive up and down
looking for a place to eat.

First, though, came checking into the room. The guy
looked at me. I looked at Lisa. I looked at the guy.

"We'd like a room." I said. No protest from Lisa, so I
continued. "Together." I checked her again, and this
time Lisa added: "With two beds."

He put out the registration forms.

"Oui, monsieur," he said.

The room was on the third floor. *Sans* toilet but *avec* shower. The head was down the hall. This was cool with me and Lisa, because the main thing was the place was clean, dry, warm, and we were together.

We parked our bags and headed downstairs to the restaurant and one of our three-and-a-half-hour meals. At this point I really was not concerning myself where this could all lead. The important thing was to have mushrooms in a light tomato sauce, steak with a pepper sauce prepared at our table, salads, champagne, cheese and fruit, and coffee.

And then, to bed.

Lisa went in the bathroom and came out in a flannel nightshirt. A really warm Canadian thing. It was white with tiny little flowers on it. She looked clean and beautiful. Always.

I went into the bathroom next and got on my trusty pajamas. We kissed and got into our respective beds. I reached up and turned off the lamp and stretched out with my eyes wide open. Then I got up and sat on the edge of my bed.

"I want to hold you," I said.

"Hold me, Michael."

I lay down next to Lisa and held her. I can only tell you there was a rush of feeling between us in that embrace. And what I was saying was honestly how I felt.

"Lisa," I whispered.

"Yes, Michael."

She was stroking my hair with one hand, and her other hand was holding the back of my neck. Her eyes were larger and softer than ever in the half-light of the room.

"Lisa, I want to hold you with nothing between us."

The flannel nightshirt and the pajamas came off.

And then the most ancient and natural and human and beautiful of all moments occurred.

Sometime that night I thought of all that had happened with us. This moment wasn't the goal. Not the way Lisa and I felt about each other. But it was part of our becoming. It was so right because this was the most important way we would now express ourselves one to another. And she was so different in this. The self-assured independent student of the Left Bank had been what? Uncertain, and tender, and physically caring in a way I could have never understood before.

For myself I was swept up in the realization of love. There were no concerns with mechanical procedures and trying to please. I had never been like this. So guided by my own feelings I could not have done anything but make her happy. That was all natural to being with Lisa. I was at once outside myself and within myself completely. I sensed her and me as one. Does it sound silly? I don't care. It was exactly how I felt. And I cried for every moment of my life before her.

There was no going right to sleep. Not until later that night. But we existed in a state of restfulness. And we spoke. Looking back, nothing serious was said. Just the gentle talk of loving. She did share something of her childhood with me. She told me how the moon could be ours.

"We have the moon in our room," she said.

I looked around and said, "Right."

She sat up and pointed to the window.

"Look, do you see the moon?" she asked.

I did see it through the window, and its light on our bed.

She told me how her mom and dad would tuck her in

when she was a little girl. And how on clear nights the moon could be seen from many of the rooms of the house. But some nights the moon would be seen through her window. That would be a special night. They would tell her the moon had come to her, to keep her company.

"Tonight the moon has come to us," she said.

I looked at her in that moonlight and I realized how I felt about this perfect girl and the profound change she had made in my life. It could be simply expressed:

"I love you, Lisa."

She touched my lips.

"I know."

She was being a little wise, but I smiled and kissed her, more gently than ever.

"How do you know?" I asked.

"Well, it's only fair," she answered softly.

Here comes the zinger. I steeled myself and asked for it.

"Why?"

"Because, Michael, I love you."

Chapter

9

THIS is really weird.

That night I had nightmares. Terrible things. I dreamed we were driving through the rain and the car went in a ditch. It seemed we kept going in and in.

Morning came and the sunlight woke me. From the window I could see the towers of Chartres Cathedral. The nightmare bugged me. It must have been some kind of guilt trip, I figured. But I couldn't see over what. Unless it was that I felt unworthy of her. Well, Christ, I could work on that. Anyway, it must have been a dream, because Lisa looked terrific. In fact, nobody should look that good in the morning. It ruins it for everybody else.

She rolled over and caught me looking at her.

"Hey, can I interest you in a tour of Chartres Cathedral?" she inquired.

Now I want to assure you I have every interest in art history. Before I got into acting, I had studied art as my major my first two years at Illinois. I even taught painting, briefly, at a community art center in Pasadena to make some money to support my acting. And as far as drawing goes, I still like to sketch, like when I'm sitting around listening to music. (This was all related to Lisa as justification for my wanting to come and see the cathedral, lest she think I had just wanted to get her into a hotel room.)

However, at that moment a new interest had arisen, as it were. And Lisa shared that interest. Besides, checkout wasn't until noon. We decided since the cathedral had been there almost eight hundred years, it would still be there that afternoon.

"Bon matin, mademoiselle et monsieur," the concierge said.

"Yipes!" we replied.

He had decided it was time for us to have breakfast. It comes with the room, right? So he knocked once and came in. (To the French—and I do bless them for this—sex really is a fact of life.) Lucky for us, and him, nothing was interrupted right at that instant. There was a certain amount of shuffling and hiding under the covers and, love it, giggling.

It was easy to make it over to the cathedral. You can see it from anywhere in Chartres. The experience of seeing the cathedral was (that overworked word does apply here) incredible. And being there with Lisa made it even more so. I mean, there was no way we couldn't think of being there then as anything but a religious experience. And it seemed right to us we were there. I know, in a way, that sounds sacrilegious, but not given the way we felt about each other; I prefer to think He would understand.

Lisa did make a big deal out of the gothic feature of using flying buttresses to support the walls so they could have lots of windows. Also, she told me about

how this was the first true High Gothic cathedral. And
then she had the nerve to claim art history was only
her minor. But what we both really fell out over were
the medieval stained-glass windows. The old way of
making them has been lost, so you just can't see this
anywhere but Europe. And to see these, with the
colored light streaming through, and the pictures of
the people who lived then, and the big kaleidoscope of
the rose window. All this, together with our love. I'll
say it again—incredible!

I did try to exercise some element of responsibility.

"We should leave, Lisa."

"Why?"

That made sense. Why the hell should we leave?
Why the hell did we have to go anywhere but where
we—it was *we* now—wanted to be?

Well, we did leave. But first we drove around and
looked at the little town of Chartres. The old part. With
medieval narrow streets on the banks of a little river.
And a stone bridge and weeping willows.

For the drive back we selected a more scenic route.
The weather was good, so we didn't see any reason to
confine ourselves to the, as they would say in L.A.,
freeway. By taking country roads we made it all the
way to Chateauneuf, which is something like fourteen
miles from Chartres.

Lisa decided we were moving too fast.

"Listen, Michael," she said, "I feel now we can talk
as friends, right?"

"Lisa, say whatever you want to say."

"Okay. Michael?"

"Yes?"

"You gotta get me something to eat," she begged.

*　*　*

There were only like about two places to eat in the whole town of Chateauneuf, a place which couldn't have had a population of more than a hundred people. One was a little inn called Le Cheval Blanc. There was a bar in the front, with some peasants (if that sounds really feudal, hell, that's what they call them) sitting around. Much farther back in the building were some benches and tables with white paper tablecloths. It wasn't exactly crowded that afternoon. Basically, we were the only people eating there.

They couldn't do enough for us.

Let's face it, we would have eaten peanut-butter sandwiches and been happy because we were doing it together. As it turned out, one more fabulous meal: baby frog legs in garlic and butter, button mushrooms, saddle of veal in a pastry crust and covered with cream sauce, and wine—another, second only to love, of the great French traditions definitely worth preserving.

We talked and ate for hours. Including desserts of fresh flavored custards.

Afterward, while we sat with wine and coffee, Lisa took a ballpoint pen from her bag and started sketching my picture on the paper tablecloth. Here I had been blabbing about my art talent before and it turns out she really drew pretty good. I mean, you could tell it was me and everything.

"Hey, Lisa, I'm the one who does the drawing."

"Then you need to learn how it feels to be a model."

I sat there loving every moment of my present existence.

"You know," I said, "I keep thinking of those people who came to Paris in the twenties—like Hemingway, and F. Scott Fitzgerald."

"Oh, yeah," Lisa said, without looking up, "I read this really good book about this couple named the Murphys, who were part of that."

"What was the title?" I asked.

"Living Well Is the Best Revenge."

I cracked up laughing. Excellent.

I tried to hold still. It felt strange to have Lisa drawing me. And that's coming from a guy who has spent a lot of time in front of the cameras. But if it felt strange, it was good realizing she was really looking at me. And what was nicer, I was looking at her.

Unfortunately, my nightmare was still lurking in my mind.

"Lisa, I got a real downer I want to bring up."

"Hold still," she said, stopping to check a line.

Worrying I would break the mood, I said, "Forget I said anything."

"Come on, Michael, what?"

"Last night I dreamed something happened to you." I paused. "Something terrible."

"Something did happen to me last night, Michael," she said, still drawing, "only it was wonderful."

Lisa put down the pen and looked at me.

"And you know something, Michael? I'd like for it to happen again. Right now."

Some things you don't have to tell me twice.

"Yes, ma'am," I said.

Immediately I went into the front bar and got a room from the manager. It was amazing how well I could communicate in French when it was really necessary. When I came back to get Lisa she showed me the drawing. It was good, damned good. And I have to say, I looked really happy—no, make that glowingly happy—in the drawing.

"Lisa," I said, "you're really good."

"So are you." She smiled.

She wrote across the bottom:

Michael Shymkus—"living well. . . ." Lisa

Right then I knew my agent was sitting with my executive producer back in Paris waiting to talk over movie deals with me before she took off for L.A., certain that was all I could be interested in. And in Scotland Wesley Crouch and Bob O'Connor were surely inventing new tortures for the last shots of the film.

But as Lisa and I headed up the stairs, all that other stuff didn't matter one little bit.

Chapter

10

IT mattered.

"Oh-oh, Lisa, I've got a message from Eve to call her."

By this time, we had worked our way back to the Westminster Hotel.

"So call her, Michael."

We went up to my room. Lisa sat down on the bed, which was a ridiculously narrow thing for a generally nice hotel, and I stood there, staring at the phone.

"But she's still here in Paris."

"Then go see her, for God's sake," Lisa said impatiently.

"That's just it," I said, getting impatient myself. "I don't want to see her."

I sat down in a chair mumbling something about why the hell couldn't Eve had gone back to Los Angeles. I mean, if it were something between me and Ron we could settle it without her. I didn't feel like dealing with her now. I wanted to be with Lisa.

"Michael?" she said, by way of getting me out of my distraction.

"Huh?"

"I don't think Eve is anywhere near as bad as you say."

Oh, Jesus. Did I need this now?

"You don't know her like I do, okay, Lisa?" I was pleading with her to drop the subject.

"In fact, Michael, I think she's pretty wonderful."

Lisa's positive assessment of Eve was no surprise to me. Hell, everyone was impressed by Eve. She worked hard, she was friendly, and she got things done. On top of that, she had come from a job as a mail sorter (she started in a television station in Philadelphia) to become one of the top agents in Hollywood. To Lisa—as to a lot of other women, I'm sure—Eve was a symbol of busting out from under and making a success. Lisa wanted to be sure I understood that.

"It couldn't have been easy for her," she pointed out. "Her work had to become her whole life."

"Lisa, that's just it—I don't want her work to become my whole life."

She thought that over and only came back stronger. "Michael, don't you see how you resent her part in your success?"

"Some success, jumping in rivers in Scotland."

"You're finally making it," Lisa insisted, "and you can't stand that you have to share it with her."

"I'm not going to share it forever!"

She had got me so riled up, I ended up telling her my big plan. How I would put up with the bitch until I could get what I wanted. And then I would do exactly as I pleased. Meaning: dropping Eve. And signing with an agent who did what I said. Okay, so it wasn't a very loyal attitude. In point of fact, it even sounded shitty to me. But this was the show biz, right?

"You want to dump Eve once you've become a big success?" Lisa asked with unhidden disgust.

"You got it," I said.

"That's really tacky, Michael."

I literally squirmed in my chair.

"I just don't want to do what I don't want to do," I tried to explain.

There was no easy way to get off the hook. Not with Miss Canadian's northern code of black-and-white issues.

"You must be good or Eve wouldn't even—"

"Being good isn't good enough in Hollywood, Lisa."

She stopped short at the interruption. I went on.

"You have to be managed," I explained. "You have to be packaged like a goddamn laundry detergent."

Lisa nodded, and practically continued my thought.

"And some things fit and some things don't?" she asked, probing.

Okay, it had crossed her mind. Where *would* she fit in?

All I could say was:

"I love you, Lisa."

She laughed. I was ready for anything but that. She got up and put her hands on the sides of my head and looked at me with those beautiful eyes.

"I know what you're thinking, Michael, but don't," she chided me. "It's just a thing—in Paris, it happens."

"No."

"Michael, you're going to leave to finish your movie and that will be that."

"Don't talk like this, Lisa."

"We've got to get back to reality."

I took her hands and held them to my lips. She was always ahead of me. Of course she knew. She always knew. But I could change all that.

"I can make it work," I said.

She saw it so much more clearly than I did. Or wanted to.

"Michael, you're a movie star and I'm a student. In

your world I'm a big zero and in my world people like you don't even really exist."

"What about our love?" I had the right to ask that.

She was shaking her head. She smiled, lovingly, fondly.

"Yeah, I've finally found him," she laughed. "Mr. Wrong."

I pulled her over to the chair and held her on my lap.

"This is different, Lisa."

"No, Michael, you don't need me holding you back, and I can't change what I am."

"What you are," and I decided to say it, as corny but, God, as truthful as it was, "is the only girl I have ever loved."

Lisa looked around the room.

"You've got a nice place here, Mike, but why is that bed so narrow?" she asked.

"I know, isn't it ridiculous?"

"Maybe," Lisa said, "but then again—it could be kind of fun."

Was it ever.

Chapter

11

EVE had me wait for her in the bar of the Tour d'Argent restaurant. It's a kind of culinary museum, seeing as how the place has been around for four hundred years. I didn't feel like drinking, so I occupied my time trying to figure out whatever Eve had to say to me tonight.

Actually, I was more than a little perturbed about any time away from Lisa. I was leaving in two days and I didn't really know when I would see her again. That was something I had to get my head around.

Finally, Eve arrived with appropriate flourishes of her Russian sable. (She loved to say it was a gift from an admirer—herself.) After a Lillet *blanc* we were shown to our table. It was by the window and the view of Paris and the Île de la Cité lit up at night was fantastic. I figured this, along with the food—which is among the best in the world—had to be some compensation for putting up with Eve Ross.

For her part, she was busy looking around to see who was there.

"I understand," she confided, "that supposedly Liz

Taylor was here last night—and just missed running into Richard Burton."

"No kidding," I said, paying far more attention to my lobster appetizer.

She then got going on the subject of the reshoot. It was her feeling I had to get on better terms with Wesley now I had made my point. In the end, he was going to cut the film. And that meant I was far more dependent on him than he on me. I told her I'd be as nice as I could but there's no way in hell I was ever going to consider myself dependent on Wesley Crouch. Or anyone else, I added.

This only provoked a dissertation from Eve on the interdependency of the filmmaking process.

I jumped as sarcastically as possible on that cue.

"Naturally, Eve, I could have never done it without you."

"You haven't done it yet, sweetheart," she snapped, "so don't kid yourself."

Fortunately at this point they showed up with our entrées. The *spécialité de maison* is duck—they literally number every duck served, like fine wine—and I was having the recommended *caneton Tour d'Argent*. No disappointment in that. So this was what it was all about: the travel, the hotels, the restaurants, the best people. And all I had to do to get it was kiss Eve's ass.

"Go fuck a duck," I muttered a little too loudly, surprising myself.

"What?"

"Uh, the duck," I covered quickly, "is very good."

"Yes, it is," she agreed, giving me a suspicious look.

Figuring we had discussed food long enough, Eve moved the conversation to business.

"I think it'd be a good idea if you go tomorrow," she advised me.

"They don't want me in Scotland until the day after," I advised her.

"Show a little extra interest," Eve said.

"I've already made plans with Lisa."

I expected Eve to rise to that. She didn't. Maybe she didn't understand the nature of my relationship with Lisa. Maybe she was just too smooth.

"The new deal looks very good," she said, seemingly dropping the subject of my leaving tomorrow. "Did you look at the script?"

I had gone over the outline, but had not read the script.

"If you like it, I like it," I said, resignedly.

"Well, one of the girls who is already signed—Alice Raymond—will be in London tomorrow."

"So?" I inquired.

"So I think it'd be smart for you to stop off and get together with her for dinner," she said, "and we can do some publicity on it."

She was too smooth.

"A little romantic interest, huh, Eve?"

"Gossip is what the public wants, Michael—give it to them."

I took a sip of wine.

"Eve, to hell with it. I'm staying here tomorrow."

"Don't give me your shit, Michael," she said. "You've got responsibilities to me and yourself that—"

"I'm seeing Lisa tomorrow!"

Eve picked up where I interrupted her.

"—that preclude a certain type of fling."

"Fling"! What a dumb-ass word. I looked around the restaurant. We were attracting attention with our debate. So what? For sure, people must have taken us for something fashionable; perhaps a fashion designer and his client. Or a kept man.

"She's not a 'fling,' okay, Eve?"

Eve leaned back in her chair and gestured European-style with her arms.

"A *divertissement,* a moment's pleasure, an interlude—once you're back in L.A. you'll forget—so let's not be silly now."

"You don't know anything about me, Eve."

"I know talent when I see it," she said, "and I don't want to see somebody throw his away."

"You're a bitch."

"No, Michael, I'm your agent."

She was so smug, thinking she had topped me.

"What's worrying you, Eve?" I teased her. "That I won't let you screw up my life?"

The waiter came and poured some more wine. We were quiet until he left.

"I worry about you, Michael."

"So you worry," I said.

"Why do you think I stayed in Paris?" she asked.

"I was wondering that myself," I said.

"O'Connor filled me in," she said. "He says you're different with this one."

Isn't it wonderful to have friends who look out for you? Good ol' Bob. I had wondered why Eve was getting so goddamn anxious.

"I guess Bob isn't so dumb about things after all," I commented.

Eve smiled. She loved the idea of having spies who kept her informed about everything. Since she had inside information, she must have felt she could be a little conciliatory.

"Look, Michael, I'm probably making too big a deal out of this."

This was her way of allowing me to slink out with grace. Well, not this time, sweetheart. Why should I let this whole thing slide? I mean, it only had to do with everything about me and what I wanted to do.

"No, Eve, you're *not* making too big a deal."

She eyed me cautiously.

"Just how serious are you?"

Eve and I, as always. Here I was being put in the position of discussing my most personal feelings. Only this concerned things that were completely private between me and Lisa. Things Lisa and I haven't even discussed.

"That's none of your goddamn business!"

I guess I really did know where my love for Lisa was taking me. Or where I wanted it to go, anyway. But did Lisa?

"Let me give you some advice, Michael," Eve said calmly. "You could have hooked up with this kind of girl six years ago when you were nothing."

Oh, Jesus, if she was going to give me the "I took you out of the gutter" sermon, I wanted to get something defined first.

"You want to tell me what you mean by 'this kind of girl,' please?" I asked.

"Michael, she is very young and nice, but"—she made a kind of a "wish I could be more helpful" gesture with her fork—"she's part of the audience, Michael; she's not like us."

"As far as I'm concerned that's in her favor," I said.

I'm sure Eve thought she was being nice about all this.

"In five years, Michael, you'll be at a place when you can do as you please about these things," she said.

"Good. That's when I dump you," I sneered.

"Honey, by then you'll have enough brains not to."

"Okay, okay, but for now I do what you say, right?" She loved me reciting that part of the lesson.

"Right."

"Wrong, Eve." I was not going to buy her crap tonight.

"Michael, don't you understand she doesn't fit in?" She sounded so reasonable, and I was so pissed off.

"Look, Eve, if I'm any good at all I don't need that publicity hype about me and young starlets and all the other bullshit!"

"She's no good for you. And what's more"—Eve was getting exasperated—"you're not good for her, either."

"I'll be the judge of that."

"You'll only hurt her."

"No way."

I could see her grinding her teeth.

"Why the hell do you want to put a weight around your neck?" she demanded.

"I already got one. You."

"You've gone flippo, pal." Me, flippo? Maybe from putting up with her shit.

"Yeah, thanks to you, Eve, dear."

Eve didn't get to the top by being sweet all the time. She decided to call in her markers.

"Look around you, Michael—what's thanks to me is this restaurant and the movie and the travel that brought you that little cunt and the next movie that'll bring you a lot more."

Oh, poor Eve, struggling for me.

"You don't make a dime, right?" I said. "You represent me as a public service."

"I represent you as long as I'm in charge, you son of a bitch, so get that straight." She had gone back to the finger-shaking routine. "And I'm telling you to dump her or I'll let you fall flat on your face!"

Eve got up and the waiters rushed to help her. She was gone in another moment. I just sat there by myself trying to figure whether I could juggle everything I had going. The hell with it—I knew what my first priority was: Lisa. Oh, but Jesus! Lisa felt the same as Eve. That we didn't belong together. Why the hell did I have all this pressure? And why did I have to keep leaving Lisa? No way! I was staying tomorrow.

They brought the check. Where was Eve now that I needed her? I started digging for cash. Okay, so now I was going to fall flat on my face, huh? Well, at least I'll do it my way.

12

Chapter

12

"YOU act like Eve's my mother or something," I said, tripping over one of the stone steps Lisa and I were climbing.

Lisa kept right on. We were in Montmartre, on our way up to the Church—or Cathedral, if you prefer—of Sacré-Coeur. It was a real climb, not made any easier by Lisa's advocacy of the cause of Eve Ross.

"Michael, she took time to stay over and talk to you."

"Yeah, about you," I reminded her.

"But you must agree I am just complicating things for you."

That was it. I stopped and grabbed Lisa and kissed her hard.

"If you're complications, Lisa, I'm glad as hell to have them set in."

We finally made it. I turned around and there was Paris: the Eiffel Tower, the Arc de Triomphe, the whole beautiful city. It was mine and Lisa's now, and yet I had to leave it. We stood looking. Taking it in.

At least we were able to get off the subject of Eve as Lisa filled me in on the history of Sacré-Coeur. She told

me how Montmartre and the hill the church is now on
was taken over during a revolt establishing the Paris
Commune in 1871. It turned out the revolutionaries
got creamed by the government. So as a kind of an
apology for making all that trouble, Sacré-Coeur was
built by donations from the common people.

It crossed my mind her speech contained a double
meaning. That I should make an apology to Eve. If so, I
preferred to carry on the revolt.

After looking around the church, we started back
through the Place du Tertre. I guess because I had
reminded Lisa that Eve wasn't my mother, she became
concerned with more familial matters.

"What about your mother?" Lisa asked.

"What about her?"

"You never talk about your parents."

What was going on here? Was I going to be psycho-
analyzed? I told Lisa my parents were fine, last time I
spoke to them. A cab came by and I grabbed it so we
could head back to my hotel. There I checked on my
calls (nothing, since Eve had left for the States), and
we went back out again. Our purpose of wandering was
not defined, except we wanted to spend time together.
Given the way we felt, and the time left until the
morning and my plane, every minute meant a hell of a
lot.

We were walking by the Madeleine, which I decided
is one of my personal favorites. It's a church built in
the design of a classic Greek temple. Lisa also mentioned
it's a favorite place for weddings, which resulted in a
long silence. I reconsidered the earlier question about
my parents.

"Hey, Lisa, I don't have any hang-ups about my
parents."

She approved with a simple "Okay."

"They live in Chicago."

"And they had you, which is the best recommendation," she added.

The truth is, I had some pretty rough battles with my parents growing up. Who doesn't? And if I wasn't fighting with them I was taking on my little brother. But some time after getting on my own, that all mellowed out. They (my folks, not my brother, who really didn't give a shit what I did) were never too crazy about my getting into acting. Even now I think they still don't know exactly what I do. Except every once in a while they hear about me, or they'll see a film or a TV show I was in. Or somebody will show them my picture from an article.

"Actually," I said, thinking about my parents as real people, "they've really got something very nice together."

Lisa didn't say anything, so I went on:

"I mean, they're like into their sixties and they're with each other and that's nice—"

Lisa was looking away from me; I wouldn't shut up.

"It should only happen to us," I said, as a wish and a prayer.

It was she who grabbed me and held me this time.

Our wanderings took us to the Seine and across the Pont Alexandre III. Lisa knew where we were going even if I didn't. Before us was Les Invalides, the group of buildings where Napoleon's tomb is. The specific place is called the Church of the Dome, as it turned out. I was about done for the day, but I perked up for this.

The tomb was huge. It kind of towered up from the floor under the dome, and the whole thing was made out of a special kind of red marble. Lisa said the French had had the stone brought from Russia. I was convinced even the most jaded studio exec would be impressed by this. On second thought, they'd probably try to buy it.

What I was thinking about was here's this great guy, Napoleon, who conquered the world, and now what? He's gone. The fancy red marble doesn't do him any good, that's for sure.

So what did this have to do with me?

The next day I would be gone. Chasing my Career. Okay, for sure I was going to see Lisa again. But at what point do I say, okay, she's what I want most—and everything else will have to get in line? (Actually, I had already decided that in my head, but I hadn't taken the full inevitable irrevocable step.) So when? And if I do go tomorrow, what about the next project? And the next?

"I'm thinking of staying tomorrow," I said.

"Don't lay that on me, Michael," Lisa said.

Would that be it? Staying because of her? Or was it staying because of myself?

"But I want to stay, Lisa."

"Right now there's more to think about than just us," she said.

She *would* think of others. And how do you really argue with her? By being selfish? That wasn't for Lisa. She was right. There were other people. I couldn't walk out on them. On a deal? Yes. On Eve? I would love to. But on the whole damn crew and the other actors and Ron Peters and O'Connor and, yes, even Wesley Crouch—no. I couldn't. Hell, that I even brought it up to Lisa made me feel so damned small.

I looked at the tomb again. Maybe there are no eternal problems. Just daily ones.

"I still think she feels motherly toward you," Lisa said, having no more to do with what I was fretting over.

"Eve again, huh?"

"I just wish you could appreciate what she does for you, Michael."

Lisa was never going to understand, that's for sure. Business is business. And business relationships are not based on emotion. That much I had learned from Eve.

"Listen, Lisa, she's not to me what Claude is to you," I said.

Well, that was the wrong thing to say. It wasn't so long ago she'd lost her own mother. Or really, for that matter, her own dad.

I mean, what I was dealing with here was a basic human need. Parents. A need I, fortunately, was being allowed the time to . . . what? If not grow out of, at least be weaned slowly from. No, that's unfair, Lisa wasn't dependent on Claude. Nothing she said indicated that. It was just, well, that she saw Eve's involvement with my life in a kind of parallel way to her own with Claude. And who was Claude? A housemother? More, I guess. A friend. Let's face it, Claude was filling a real place for her. For now anyway, that was the right thing.

But why did I have to bring up Claude in the first place? I mean, it only gave Lisa an idea.

"Michael, I want you to meet Claude."

"When I come back—" I began.

"Michael." Lisa looked at me and I found myself looking away, talking to the wall.

"She's probably busy," I suggested, "and we really should get ourselves some dinner and—"

"Why don't you want to meet Claude?" Lisa asked.

On the way over to meet Claude, I went through my hesitancy about meeting the French woman. Number one, she might not think much of Lisa's relationship with me. For number two, see number one. I mean, you've got to realize Lisa had filled Claude in on who she was spending time with (she assured me she had left out the details—"But she is French," Lisa reminded me), and for sure Claude had her own ideas about who was right for Lisa.

Note: I was convinced I was not good enough for Lisa—a frame of mind I was certain would be shared by anyone who knew her.

Just think how it looked.

Here's this actor from Hollywood I met. We've spent a lot of time together while he's in Paris. Soon he'll leave, but I'm sure he'll be back.

It sounded fishy even to me.

"What'd Claude say when you told her our, uh, situation?" I asked.

We were in a cab on our way out to La Maison Canadienne. It was at 31 Boulevard Jourdan, which took us by the Montparnasse cemetery (this was turning out to be a real cheerful day) and on to the Porte d'Orléans, which is practically by the Boulevard Périphérique expressway which rings Paris.

"She said she was happy for me."

"Like that?"

"No, she said it in French," Lisa said, reminding me again of something she had already told me. "We speak French to each other."

Okay, so Claude was happy. *Happy*? Maybe she was happy because she thought it wouldn't last? You know, a "fling." (Oh, God, there's Eve's word again.) Would she be so happy when she sees I'm serious? How is she going to see I'm serious? I mean, what am I supposed to do? I should have met her a lot earlier—there wouldn't have been all this worry.

"Did you tell her I'm an actor?"

"Of course, Michael. Is that a secret?"

"What'd she think of that?"

"She thought it was interesting."

Aha! *Interesting.* Now it comes out. Hates actors. Thinks they're irresponsible. Or worse, thinks I've only made it up to impress Lisa. No, Lisa must have told her about the meeting with Eve and everybody. Oh, Christ! How did that sound? She must think we're all bonkers, for sure. No wonder she must believe Lisa and I aren't really serious.

Otherwise, she'd tell Lisa to dump me.

"Does she know I'm leaving tomorrow?" I asked.

"Yes," Lisa answered.

"What'd she say?"

"She said she'd like to meet you before you go."

Before I could say anything else, Lisa added, "Here we are."

Let's see . . . Claude said, *"Before I go."* That probably meant she really didn't think I would be back. On the other hand, she did want to meet me. Would she have wanted to meet me if she didn't think we were serious? Or was she only being polite?

"You worry too much," Lisa said, getting out of the cab.

If there were a contest for Miss Maison Canadienne surely Lisa would have won it. People—good-looking Canadian guys and gals—came up to her to talk and laugh. Were all Canadians so handsome or pretty as these seemed? Of course not, but to me everything surrounding Lisa was a wonder.

Everything, that is, except me.

I kind of tagged along. I shook some hands, did some nodding to others. If Lisa was showing me off that day, it was I who was the one being impressed. If only she could have waited until the movie was released. Maybe then I would get a little more recognition.

One of the girls was staring at me.

"I've seen you on television back home," she said.

Finally! I smiled, but before I could say anything Lisa chimed in:

"I didn't know you watched Saturday-morning cartoons."

Lisa smiled while I got out of that one.

What I did was hand out some general bullshit about acting and my current film. Lisa was patient enough to let me get through it for at least a minute.

The worst was meeting the guys. Nice guys and all that, but I didn't particularly care for Lisa to have that many distractions. Some of them really *were* good-looking. And they treated Lisa terrifically (could anyone be any other way?) in a kind of easy camaraderie. I even learned there had been a guy in Ottawa who wanted to follow her from Canada, but gave up when he saw it was a lost cause. Whatever, all these Canadians were here together and they were all looking out for one another. It was really a nice thing.

Oh my God! If they thought the same awful things about me that Claude probably did, I was going to get my ass kicked!

"Monsieur Gourgueshon," Lisa called, and to me said, "Here, I do want you to meet our maintenance man."

This must have been the backup team, in case I could handle the Canadians. I didn't think Frenchmen got that big. He looked right from Central Casting—blue work clothes and a beret stuck up on his head. We smiled at each other. I up at him, he down at me. Lisa filled him in on what I was doing there (I would have loved a translation for my own benefit), at which point he gave me a couple of friendly whacks on the shoulder. I figured if he ever wanted to get out of janitoring, he could always get a job as a trained bear.

"Oh, Michael, he says you should know you're with a wonderful girl," she informed me.

"Please tell him I'm very aware of that," I said.

"I already did."

We went down a hallway and knocked on a door.

"Entrez!"

I fell for Claude Saché instantly. I had imagined she would be a feeble little old lady. Okay, she was old, no, let's say advanced in years or something, but she was really good-looking with it. She had long light-gray hair which she wore pulled together at the back of her neck and hanging down from there. Her body was still slim, like an ex-dancer (which, it turned out, she was), and although her face had lines, they worked great on her.

She extended her hand and I shook it. It crossed my mind to kiss it, but I was sure Lisa would crack up.

"Asseyez-vous là, s'il vous plaît," Claude said, motioning to a chair.

Lisa started to translate, but even I understood I was supposed to sit down. After I did, Lisa went to a cabinet and poured us all a glass of Pernod. I sipped mine with a smile. Not that I'm particularly crazy about the stuff, but you never would have known it that day.

They began speaking to each other in French. I could see a kind of reverence in Lisa's eyes toward Claude. I could also figure I was being covered in the conversation, because they were laughing and looking over to me. Meanwhile, I became aware of classical music playing. It was a record player with some violin concerto on. The room where we were was not large. I could see a couple of rooms off it, what looked like a bedroom and a little kitchen.

There were some paintings and prints on the walls of the living room, so I got up and started looking at them. Lisa came over to me.

"This one," she told me, "is a Matisse etching."

It was a mother and child, done with only six lines in the whole thing—perfectly placed.

"And this," Lisa went on, "is a Rouault lithograph—both men were friends of Claude's."

"Would you mind very much if I fall in love with Claude, too?" I asked.

"Why not? I love you both," Lisa said.

We sat down again. I asked Lisa to tell Claude everything about her was beautiful and I was very happy to be here. Lisa did and translated Claude's reply.

"She says you are a wonderful flatterer, but she will accept your compliments, anyway."

"Merci," I said, really proud I was able to speak directly in French.

Claude said something back to me in French and I didn't understand a word. Again I looked to Lisa.

"She says even without my exaggerations about how wonderful you are, you're all right."

Did I detect a compliment? Of course, Claude was going to be nice to me around Lisa. No, I figured she wouldn't if she didn't mean it. She didn't seem that way. As for me, all I could do was be myself. What more could I do?

Claude spoke again, and Lisa turned to me.

"What'd she say now?" I asked, anxiously.

"She said you should stop worrying about making a good impression."

So what did I do? Right. I kept trying to impress her.

I swear I meant every word when I raised my glass and said:

"May every moment be as beautiful as this one."

Lisa shook her head at me.

"Pretty drippy, but I'll pass your line on, anyway."

She did, and laughed at Claude's comment.

"Claude says you're very sentimental, but since you are leaving tomorrow she'll put up with it."

Oh, Jesus—I was making a total fool of myself. Screw it. I was filled with a romantic grandeur.

"Please tell Claude I just have to get some acting commitments straightened out and I'll be back."

She listened politely to Lisa's translation.

"Oui." Claude smiled. *"Et si ma tante en avait elle s'appellerait mon oncle."*

Lisa laughed. Okay, girls, how about letting me in on the gag?

"C'mon, Lisa, pass it on."

"It's kind of colloquial," she said.

"Don't give me that grammar crap, what'd she say?"

Lisa took my hand and glanced over at Claude.

"She says, basically, it's very nice you feel this way but"—Lisa paused for a moment, before continuing—"if her aunt had balls, she'd be her uncle."

I kind of just sat there for a moment looking at my drink. Then I slowly started to laugh. They both joined me. I leaned forward to Lisa, and gestured toward Claude.

"Ask your friend what she's doing for dinner tonight."

We decided to head back to the St. Germain-des-Prés district on the Left Bank, to a place Lisa had mentioned to me before. It was the Café Procope. This is a really old restaurant, dating from the middle of the seventeenth century. Lisa explained its claim to fame was that Voltaire used to hang out there. I figured if it was good enough for Voltaire, I shouldn't complain.

All that aside, Lisa and Claude wanted to go there. Probably because it wasn't expensive. That was only part of it—the other part was it's just a good place to eat. And there were lots of students there, too.

It turned out they had some of the new Beaujolais wine. This was a find. We got into that real good that night. I was in a kind of half-dream, looking at Lisa, and trying not to think about having to leave tomorrow.

A gal Lisa knew from school came over and started talking to her about the political campaign. Claude turned to me and said in English:

"When I met you I am thinking of asking you a question," she said.

I swallowed a marinated artichoke heart whole.

"You speak English?"

"Is very hard for me," Claude said, "but I am saying something."

"Whatever you want, madame, or ma'am."

"I am thinking before of asking if you love Lisa," she said in her accent. "Now I see you do."

I looked over at Lisa, talking to her friend.

"I do love her," I said to Claude.

The other girl went back to her table. Lisa kiddingly accused Claude and me of cutting her out.

"I see you two don't need me any more."

"Well, Claude was holding out on me," I said. "She speaks English."

Claude put up her hands.

"No, no," she protested, "my English is, uh, *en anglais, comment dit-on 'merdique'?*"

"*Merdique?* That'd be 'shitty', Claude," answered Lisa.

"*Oui.* My English is shitty," said Claude proudly.

I looked at Lisa.

"What kind of English are you teaching Claude?"

"The kind you understand." Lisa winked.

Lisa and I were holding hands on the table. Claude reached across and put her hand on top of ours.

"It is very wonderful tonight, no?" she said.

"Yes," I said, "and there will be other nights."

Lisa looked at me but didn't say anything.

"You are children," Claude said, "but you are asking to grow up."

Lisa spoke to Claude in French.

"No fair, Lisa," I warned her.

"I told her we're enjoying ourselves now—not to worry about the future," Lisa said. In the warm light of the restaurant I could see her eyes were wet.

No one said anything for what seemed a long time. Maybe the wine had settled us down. Or maybe it made me bold, because I decided it was time for action. As if I could physically stop the moment I leaned over and kissed Lisa. At first hard and then very softly. People around stopped talking. When we finished I looked at Claude. She had raised her glass to us.

"*À l'amour*," she said, and nearby tables joined in the toast.

I saw Claude smile. And I saw tears in her eyes, too.

We got back to La Maison Canadienne and put Claude into her room. There was no doubt she would sleep well tonight, thanks to the *Beaujolais nouveau*.

Lisa held her finger to her lips for me to be quiet. I followed her up the stairs to what turned out to be her room.

She opened the door and I followed her inside. To me it was the *sanctum sanctorum*—the holiest of places.

We sat with just her desk lamp on and whispered. Lisa showed me pictures of her father. He was tall, in the uniform of a Canadian army officer, and above all, young. And there were pictures of her mother. It was impossible to tell from which side Lisa's beautiful eyes came from, but her face definitely favored her mother's. (I also saw if her mother was any indication, Lisa would not lose her beauty—although I honestly had never doubted that.)

Oh yes. Little Mikey, the toy lion, was there. Right on Lisa's pillow.

"Michael, do you know why I never brought you here before?" Lisa asked, still in a whisper.

"I thought it was against the rules or something," I said, kind of curious.

"I wasn't sure I could take having memories of you where I sleep."

We made sure the memories of that night were good ones.

Chapter

13

THERE'S a little bar at the back of the George Hotel in Inveraray. The walls are all rough stone from two centuries ago when the place was a church. When it's cold, which is most of the time in Scotland, they keep a fire going.

Ron Peters was enjoying the fire and his second scotch, but he was not enjoying our conversation.

"You sure you aren't just tired from this picture, Michael?"

"Yes, I am tired, but that's not it."

We were the only people there except for the bartender. Ron decided he could use a third scotch, so he went over and got it. This might take a fourth and a fifth; besides.

He sat down and politely continued our "talk."

"What is it, then?" He punctuated that with a kind of sigh that intimated he had a million better things to do than screw around with me.

"I just don't want to go right into the next project."

"You're shittin' me."

"No, I'm not."

"Eve has convinced me you're right for the part," he reminded me.

"It's not up to her, Ron." Why the hell did I feel uncomfortable using his first name?

"Isn't Eve your agent?"

"As far as I'm concerned—no."

Ron ran his fingers over his face, scratching his chin and ruminating about what I was saying. He looked down at his drink as he spoke.

"Listen, Michael, I think the picture we're doing now is going to be very big for you. And me."

Who's talking about this picture? I was talking about the next one.

"I have no doubts about what we're doing," I said. "Especially with the reshoot."

"So now's the time to capitalize on success," said Executive Producer Ron Peters. "You need Eve for that."

"Look, it's just that right now—"

"And believe me, I'd be happy not to be dealing with Eve," he rolled right on. "She can be a real bitch."

"You're telling me? It's just—"

"But I hate to see you fuck yourself up."

Right. Better I should let him and Eve do it for me.

"Hey, will you listen to me for a minute?" I insisted. "I don't need Eve to talk for me."

He put his drink down and looked at me.

"You want to negotiate without Eve?"

"I want some time—I just don't want to get into another project right away."

I think I got his attention.

"What about your publicity commitments on this picture?"

Oh, yes. I was supposed to run around the country and do talk shows and stuff to push the picture. That really sounded like a lot of crap all of a sudden.

"I don't know."

"What do you mean, you don't know?"

How many ways can I try to get across the same thing?

"I want some time to think."

Ron shook his head.

"Your contract says you do publicity, Michael. If you don't, I don't pay," he said, without raising his voice one bit. "Now how do you like negotiating on your own?"

I turned in my chair to face Ron completely. I was so furious I didn't care what I said.

"Listen, there's more important things than your goddamn money! I asked you for some time to think and yes or no I'm taking it and I really don't give a shit what it costs me."

I started for the door. The bartender discreetly started washing glasses. Ron sat looking at the fire.

"Hey, Mike."

It was Ron. I stopped at the door.

"Is this all about that girl you met in Paris?"

I refused to answer that, so he continued.

"Michael, we're going to London when we finish up here," Ron told me. "Have her meet you, rest up a week on expense account, take a car and driver—whatever you want. Then we'll talk it over again."

The son of a bitch! Why'd he have to be so goddamn reasonable?

I knew by the time I got to London I would be totally wrecked. We had been turning in fourteen-hour days to hold costs down on the reshoot.

But you'd better believe I had enough energy to call

Lisa so I could tell her the benefits of a week with me in London.

I waited while they got her from her room and she came to the phone.

"Lisa, how'd you like a free trip to come see me in London?"

"I wouldn't," she announced.

What? How the hell was it supposed to work out if she wouldn't let it? And after I just laid myself out to Ron Peters. Could something have happened? The elections weren't for a while. God! Why did I humiliate myself like this?

"Okay, Lisa, I guess I made a mistake."

She spoke softly, almost a whisper.

"Really what I would like is to buy my own ticket to London—and come see you."

Great kidder, that Lisa. Let her have her fun. Since the object of my calling was to get her to London, I chalked this one up as a win.

Waldenbooks

```
0449143821 2  1 @  1.95        1.95

                    SUBTOTAL   1.95
WISCONSIN 4% TAX                 .08
                       TOTAL   2.03
                     PAYMENT   2.03

                      CHANGE    .00
```

THANK YOU - PLEASE COME AGAIN

Chapter

14

THE second thing we did after Lisa showed up at the Churchill Hotel was decide where to go for supper.

I wanted to do something really English, but I also wanted to make sure we enjoyed the food, too. Not an easy task. Where I came out was Wheeler's in London's Soho district, which has fresh Dover sole prepared umpteen different ways—about seventy percent of which are incredible.

Lisa and I decided to get all duded up for the evening. I did this designer suit and she had this fantastic dress. I mean, she had this dynamite green velour dress with matching tie belt she looked fantastic in. Anyway, we figured we had to get dressed up to go out, right?

The truth is we could have both done with a nap. That's right—a nice twenty-minute first-grader roll-out-the-mats nap. I was wiped out from the shooting schedule; Lisa was coming off some heavy late nights studying for exams combined with working on Thomer's campaign. But no, you don't come to London to sleep.

Not with an expense account and a chauffeured Rolls-Royce.

Besides, I was out to show Lisa (no, really, I was out to show myself) what Hollywood money could buy. After all, this is what I was thinking of giving up.

When we got to the lobby the chauffeur was waiting. Fabulous. Lisa didn't even see me nod to him to bring the car up. I left word with the desk where we'd be, in case Ron or Bambi needed to get hold of me, and we went outside.

In front of us was a Rolls-Royce Silver Cloud with the door open. Naturally, Lisa was looking around for a taxi.

"What are you doing, Lisa?" I asked. "Get in."

"Yeah, sure," she said. "Very funny."

"Okay." I got in and pulled Lisa after me. "Terrence, take us to Wheeler's in Soho."

While we rode I showed off the built-in bar.

"Goddamn," Lisa said, in her best American hillbilly imitation, "this hyar's a right fancy car."

In front of Wheeler's, I told Terrence we'd be about two hours. He said he'd be waiting when we came out. Ah, the decadence of it all. They sat us in one of the upstairs rooms, where we got into oysters from the English Channel, the famous Dover sole, and lots of other good things, including strawberries covered with double Devon cream. That's thick, rich, instant-heart-attack-type cream. Excellent!

About halfway through the maître d' came to our table and announced I had a call from Beverly Hills, California.

"I knew I shouldn't have left word where I'd be."

"Go on, Mr. Hollywood," Lisa said.

Guess who was on the phone? You got it: Eve. Fortunately, I had already downed a glass of wine.

"Hey, Eve," I screamed, even though the connection was pretty good. "How they hanging, baby?"

"You asshole, Michael, what the hell did you tell Ron Peters?"

She was really pissed.

"I told him if he wanted something from me he should talk to me."

"What? Speak up!"

There was not a single reason in the world for me to be nervous around Eve at that point. But I was.

"I told him to deal with me direct . . . for now."

"Michael, you're going to screw things up."

I really didn't feel like some bullshit long-distance lecture.

"Oh, Eve?"

"Yes?"

"Bye."

I hung up and went back to the table.

"Three guesses who called," I announced.

"Eve, Eve, and Eve," she said.

I ordered Lisa not to get into the subject. But it was still bugging me, so I decided it was time for a little *après*-dinner pick-us-up.

"How about a little Madeira, my dear-a?"

"I've heard that one, Michael."

"Okay, then let's make it port, sport."

Terrence (I meant to speak to him about that name) was waiting for us when we got downstairs. The most sensible thing, Lisa suggested, was for us both to get some sleep.

I let her know as patiently as possible that since we had a chauffeur and a Rolls at our disposal, we were out for the night, goddammit.

"Michael," she said, holding my hands tightly, "I enjoy myself just being with you."

"But don't you understand, Lisa, we're high rollers tonight."

High Rollers. That was it. I had completely forgotten London had gambling casinos. The catch was you had to be a member for a day or so before they'd let you in. This is to avoid spur-of-the-moment gamblers like myself. Not to worry. It turned out Terrence used to drive for a place called the Silver Saddle Club. He took us there and talked them into letting us in. A few ten-pound notes didn't hurt, either.

Let me be the first to tell you the Silver Saddle Club is not London's classiest casino. Or even the second-classiest. But it was fine for our purposes. There were big chandeliers and lots of red plush. The croupiers were all in tuxedos, and here's the big number: you could shoot good old American craps.

I mean, as much as I felt I was doing the James Bond bit that night, I really didn't want to sit around and play chemin-de-fer.

The first thing I did, making sure Lisa saw me do it, was give Terrence some money to do some playing himself. Next I got a pile of chips and started out with blackjack. That got me nowhere fast. I turned to Lisa.

"Come on," I said, rubbing my palms together. "I'll show you some real action."

We walked up to the craps table, which had a pretty good crowd already. Now I have to tell you, as superficial and tawdry as all this sounds, it was a supremely great superficial and tawdry moment.

By the time I got in between some people, the dice came to me.

You have to understand I am not a big gambler. I don't even consider myself a little gambler. But I've done the weekend scene in Vegas once in a great while and it's fun and that's it. So there I was, standing with dice in my hand, in this London casino.

"Okay, high roller," Lisa said, getting into it. "Go get 'em."

I rolled thirteen straight passes!

Lisa's eyes were as big as silver dollars, or silver pounds or whatever.

And all the time the croupier was announcing to people, "This is the table, ladies and gentlemen—it's the American's game—better get in on it." And across from me there was a little Peter Lorre type, counting, "Why, that's his seventh pass . . . that's his eighth pass . . ."

More people were crowding around. I heard someone yell, "The Yank's hot!"

Okay, I should have won a small fortune. But the truth is I was really getting self-conscious and nervous. As a result I didn't manage my money at all. Just kind of threw it on, taking some off and that kind of thing. One of the biggest bets I made was on the fourteenth roll, and it hurt a lot. In spite of all that, there were piles of chips and cash in front of me. I mean, a real haul. Without uttering a single word, I started scooping it up—dumping some into the pocket Lisa made by pulling her dress up and the leftovers into Terrence's cap.

We had to walk all the way across the room to the cashier, where I received a few thousand pounds in exchange. Then followed one of my great scenes. With Lisa holding my arm and my chauffeur behind me, and a rather blasé expression on our faces, we walked back across the entire casino to leave. People actually stopped playing to look at us.

Now throughout all of this, none of the three of us spoke. Not a word. Terrence got our coats and we went down to the first floor. The Rolls was parked right in front. It was only after we were all inside the car I said my first words.

I began beating the seat and flopping around and screaming:

"Did you see what I did? Wooo-ey! Yow! Am I fantastic? Ayiyiyiyiyiyiyi! Wow! Me!"

Lisa looked over at me and said in a dry made-up British accent:

"Well, Michael, you're really quite pleased with yourself, aren't you?"

She smiled, and it went into a laugh. And then she leaped on me. It's a good thing for the Rolls and Terrence it wasn't that long of a ride back to the Churchill.

And yet, something wasn't right. Honestly. I was trying too damned hard.

We were up at five-thirty the next morning to make an early screening with Ron Peters and Wesley and O'Connor. The whole deal was set up so Ron could see the new footage and get to New York.

It was the first time Lisa had been officially introduced to Ron, and he treated her with extra courtesy. She was just wearing jeans and this comfortable suede cowhide blazer over a checked shirt and a V-neck pullover. All in all, she was very relaxed about the whole thing. He got her coffee and asked her to sit next to him. (This really destroyed Bambi.)

I sat next to Lisa, putting her between Ron and me.

"Roll 'em, Bambi," Ron commanded.

The dailies from Scotland had everything we were missing before. It was also a chance for Lisa, and everyone else, to see I wasn't bullshitting about needing the extra shots. I mean, there was the picture up on the screen. And it worked.

"You are pretty wonderful," Lisa whispered, squeezing my thigh.

Pause.

"Dammit," she added.

When it was over, everybody started splitting for where they had to be. Wesley Crouch was going back to Los Angeles and take a few days or so before he started working with the editor. O'Connor was going along to take care of post-production details. Bambi was on her way to New York with Ron.

I shook hands all around. Now that it was pretty much wound up with me, even Wesley was all sugar.

Ron said goodbye to Lisa. He also checked on how I was enjoying myself.

"Everything's terrific, Ron," I replied.

"You see," he said, "all it takes is money."

I guessed that was supposed to be a joke.

"Have a good trip," I said.

"Yeah, and I'll be seeing you for the publicity, Michael," he yelled back, as he and Bambi went off. "We've got a big hit here."

I was trying to make up my mind whether I should run after Peters to set him straight, although I *was* wavering, when Lisa gave a tug on my arm.

"Alone at last," she said.

My mind was on other, more expensive things.

"C'mon, Lisa baby, I'm taking you to Harrods," I announced. "It's practically a national treasure."

Lisa didn't seem that excited. That was okay, I was sure she'd come around when we got there. After all, Harrods department store was the *pièce de résistance* on the Michael Shymkus tour of London. And besides, it wasn't like we were walking in there without money, right?

I had Terrence drop us off at the entrance to Harrods' food halls. This, I wanted Lisa to understand, is the only real way to come into Harrods. The sight of those vast, high-ceilinged, tiled rooms, one after another, filled with game, and imported and English-prepared and beautifully displayed foods, is guaranteed to cause gout just from looking.

"Look at this humongeous amount of food!" Lisa exclaimed, at the rows of hanging rabbits and pheasants and grouse. "I could gain weight just walking through here."

"You see, Lisa, it's the little things in life that count," I philosophized. "Chauffeured limousines, private gambling clubs, wild game, delicacies . . ."

We worked our way along the pâté section, getting tastes of every variety. Then over to the cheeses. Finally, we found ourselves out of the food department.

"Okay," Lisa said, "now where do you want to go?"

"Lunch."

"Lunch? Michael, you gotta be kidding."

I took her hand.

"Just a sandwich or something," I said, heading for the elevators, "right here at Harrods."

We found a cafeteria, which seemed like a pretty good choice for right then. I talked Lisa into a small salad and a cup of coffee. I managed an open-faced sandwich.

As it turned out, we didn't even really want that. But since it was about one o'clock, it seemed proper to me we should eat. So we sat there, nibbling, and we found ourselves silent.

Well, so what? I mean, we couldn't just talk all the time. Why the hell couldn't we? Except that I had nothing to say. And obviously neither did Lisa. Funny, we could have anything and we were just sitting. Maybe she was tired. We had been running pretty hard. Okay, it was time to move on.

"You finished?" I asked.

She nodded.

"Okay, come on," I said, starting to get up.

Lisa didn't move. I sat back down.

"Mike, what are you trying to prove?"

"Nothing," I said. "I just want you to enjoy yourself." I thought a moment, and explained further, "That's what money's for."

She looked as if she hadn't quite gotten the idea yet. After a few moments, she smiled wryly.

"Okay, you're the tour guide, what's next on the itinerary?" Lisa asked, finishing her coffee. "Supper?"

"You're not pooping out on me, are you, Lisa?"

"Lead on," she said, managing a tired smile.

I got the check and we went out into the store again.

"Where are you taking me, Michael?"

"You'll see."

We lurched to the department where the young women's clothes are. Lisa stayed right beside me. I started looking through the racks. Pretty soon I had pulled out a skirt and a couple of blouses I thought she'd go for.

"Listen, Michael," she was pleading with me, "don't you want to get some sleep?"

She wasn't catching on at all.

"Lisa, don't you want me to buy you some clothes?"

Now I saw the hands go to the hips.

"Oh, Michael," she said, shaking her head, "looks like you've let the cat out of the bag."

Escalation. I suppose I should say I was overtired. Or that I felt ridiculous standing there holding women's clothing. But the fact is I must never excuse the way I acted.

"What's the matter, Miss freak broad, you too god-damn pure to let me buy you anything?"

"You bastard, everything isn't for sale!"

Let me say I am not given to public demonstration.

Let me also say I consider myself to have behaved like a total asshole at that moment. Recognizing that in no way forgives what I did, just proof that I know how rotten it was.

I threw the clothes at her feet.

"Okay, Lisa! You got yourself here, you can get yourself home!"

I looked around at the other people in the store staring at us. Correction, at me. Because when I looked back, Lisa was gone.

I didn't take the time to feel foolish. I just left the clothes on the floor and ran off to the elevators. Nothing. I went down the stairs, thinking that would save time. The whole situation felt hopeless.

On the first floor, I started going through department after department. The food halls? No luck. How could she just disappear in a store?

Some manager type literally grabbed me as I ran by.

"May I help you?" he asked.

"I'm looking for my—" my what? I couldn't say fiancée—and she was more than a girl friend, or so I hoped, anyway. Shit! "My companion is lost, a girl, twenty-two."

He must have thought I was really crazy. He had a cop—pardon me, a bobby—come over and get the description. I babbled something about her being beautiful and angry and frightened. Christ! This was just wasting time. I thanked them and tried to leave. The bobby wanted to see my passport. I had to concoct a story just to get away from them.

She must have gone back to the hotel.

The driver got me to the Churchill as fast as he could. I was screaming at him to hurry. I had never seen so much fucking traffic. Shit! I could have walked faster.

At the hotel there were cars lined up letting people

off. I didn't even wait until we stopped. I jumped out and ran along the walk and through the entrance door. A quick check around the lobby. Just people having tea. I must have appeared really weird, because they were giving me suspicious looks. Forget them.

I had to find Lisa.

Of course, the room! Goddamn those elevators. When one finally came I pushed in front of some people and got on first. I stood right at the doors and jumped off on our floor. *Our* floor. I ran down the hall to the room.

Her bag was gone.

I called Air France to see if she had made a reservation. Forget it. No trace. Nothing on British Airways either. It occurred to me she wouldn't have stopped to call.

There was only one thing to do. Go the hell out to the airport and see. It was a long shot, but where else?

I've blown it. Oh, please. God, no.

Terrence did what he could. Jesus, I mean, here's this Rolls-Royce on the expressway weaving in and out, changing lanes, the whole thing.

We got to Heathrow in fairly decent time. Big deal. Now do I start running all over the fucking airport? There were three buildings. She must be gone by now. That is, if she were ever there in the first place.

"Let's try Air France first," I said.

We pulled up and I jumped out and ran in.

There were lots of people. Crap! It seemed the whole world had suddenly decided to use this terminal. I started checking the lines of passengers at the ticket counters. No Lisa.

I crowded in at Air France and asked them if she was on the passenger list. They told me to wait my turn. I didn't want to get bogged down with an argument. Ah, the phone booths.

I checked every one of them. Nothing.

This was it. I was out of ideas. Since I was standing by the phones, I put through a call to the Churchill. That was a waste. There were no messages for me.

I started walking back to the entrance to the terminal. It was really kind of silly now. Oh, I could go to British Airways to see if she took their flight, but what was the difference. She was gone.

As I reached the door to leave I turned and looked over the terminal. There were so many people. Long lines. And there were the stairs to customs.

That's where I saw Lisa.

She was going up the stairs to customs.

"Lisa!"

She stopped.

I was running. Bouncing off of people and pushing through lines. She was standing there with her bag on those stairs and I was going to get to her no matter what.

It's a wonder I didn't knock anyone down. I broke through a last group of travelers and got to the stairs. She was looking at me, not moving.

I climbed to within a few steps of her. If I ever needed to say the right thing I needed to now. But the great creative genius was afraid to speak. So I just stood there looking up at her.

She did the speaking for me. She said so quietly I could barely hear her, "Our love belongs in Paris."

I went up a couple of more steps. When I was close enough I put my arms around her waist and kind of collapsed to my knees holding her for all I was worth. It really didn't matter who was watching or where we were any more. All that mattered was being with Lisa. *All*.

The rest was easy. I put the ticket on my American Express card and went through British emigration with no baggage. Oh, yes, but first I gave Terrence a big tip and sent him off. And throughout the whole process of leaving England I refused to let go of Lisa's hand.

In twenty minutes we had taken off from Heathrow.

As we started to level off, Lisa put her head on my shoulder. Then she looked up at me for a second.

"How are we doing now?" she asked.

"I think we're going to be all right," I replied.

"I think so, too," she said.

Paris would make everything right again.

Chapter

14

IT is not as though you can bounce into Paris and get a room at the George V.

Which would have been absolutely wrong for us anyway. After the farce I put us through in London none of the pseudo-opulence of the George V was necessary.

So there we were, riding the moving walkway in one of the glass tubes at Charles de Gaulle airport, and figuring we'd just as soon take our chances on finding a room.

What that meant was a cab ride to the Gare de Lyons railroad station. Why the Gare de Lyons? Because there are always lots of little hotels right by the train stations in Europe. And one of them was bound to be able to put us up.

That's what we got. A teeny room by the Gare de Lyons. At only the third place we tried. It had a little elevator that was really an open cage big enough for one and a half people. The concierge insisted it worked most of the time. If that was the case, then it only worked when we were in our room.

What it added up to was four floors walking. On the way up, I mumbled something about moving to L'Hôtel in the morning.

"Shall we take it?" I inquired of Lisa, having sent the concierge away.

She looked around the room. Most of it was taken up by a twin bed. There was even a neon sign to be seen through the window.

"Do we have a choice?" Lisa countered.

"I mean, is it enough?"

Lisa looked around the room again.

"Well, Michael, you're here and I'm here," she said as if I hadn't realized it. "And I couldn't care diddly-squat about anything else."

She sat down on the bed and scrunched her back up against the headboard.

"By the way," Lisa said, changing the subject completely (as usual), "you never asked me about my social life while you were in Scotland."

Oh-oh, tread carefully, Michael.

"I figured it was none of my business."

Actually, I didn't want to think about that too much. Shit, it wasn't as if we were apart all that long of a time. On the other hand, she was alone and beautiful and very desirable. Certainly she met lots of guys at the political rallies.

"Aren't you curious?" Lisa asked.

"Goddammit, of course I'm curious," I replied.

She said nothing. I fidgeted a bit, and spit out the question:

"Okay, how the hell was your so-called social life?"

"Lonely."

Lisa was sitting on the bed with her legs pulled up under her. The light from the neon sign illuminated one side of her face. The gold in her hair shone. The strange thing was, here we were in this tacky little room and because of Lisa's presence there wasn't anything tacky about it. Jesus, did she look good.

"Whadja say?" I asked.

"I said I've been lonely."

"You mean, you and I, too, the same—" I garbled. "I hoped—"

"Right, lover," Lisa said, slipping off her sweater, "but if you had asked me I would have never told you."

I sat, not moving, enjoying my view of Lisa.

"Hey, Michael?"

"Yeah, Li—"

"I hope you didn't come here just to talk."

Let me say there was a whole lot of loving going on in that room.

Lisa and I were very basic about our needs. Sex, thirst, and hunger.

It was finally time for thirst and hunger.

We walked over to the Gare de Lyon, where there was a big ornate restaurant. That's right, a great restaurant in a train station; that's Paris. It's called Le Train Bleu. I can't tell you anything about the food, because by the time we showed up they weren't serving, even though some people were still finishing up. However, the ambience looked great. Real Belle Époque. In that way it was like Chez Denis, except this place was far fancier. Oh, Le Train Bleu had already achieved national-monument status. So what we did was kind of walk around and look the place over. Besides, the few people still dining didn't seem to care. Maybe they were even flattered.

Out in front of the station, we looked around for a backup spot. There was a place catty-corner, a brasse-

rie named La Tour de Lyon. We crossed the street and I
checked to make sure they were open.

"Okay, we can get a table here," I came out and told
Lisa. "That is, if you like the place."

She gave me a look.

"Me? What about you?"

"Really, it's up to you," I said.

She brushed by me, heading inside.

"You nut," she said, shaking her head, "I'm flashing
on us being eighty-nine years old saying to each
other"—and she did this little old lady's voice—" 'how
about this restaurant, gramps?' 'Gee, I dunno, whaddya
think, granny?' "

What really floored me is it was the first time Lisa
actually allowed as how we might be together when we
were eighty-nine years old. I liked the idea immensely.

Lisa always maintained you could flop down anywhere in Paris and get a good meal. La Tour de Lyon
was no exception. We settled in for the next couple of
hours over onion soup and salad Niçoise and some very
good Bordeaux wine.

Sometime after the first hour it occurred to me I was
totally relaxed.

"You know, I kind of watch how I act with other
people," I admitted, for no particular reason except I
was with the woman I loved.

"It's always like that," Lisa agreed. "People expect
something of you and you find yourself playing to it."

"You've done that?" I asked.

"At times," she answered.

"I thought I was the actor," I smiled.

"Not the only one. You're just getting paid for it."

I poured a little wine. She was touching on something that had always bugged me in my life—being myself.

"Lisa, I'm myself with you," I said. "I don't feel there's some other way I should be acting."

"I know," Lisa said. "I haven't had to be anybody else for you, either."

Lisa got what I would call a far-away-back-home-in-Canada kind of look.

"You see, Michael, everyone is looking at us through a lot of crap," she said. "Like who we were in high school or grade school or with our parents or something."

"Or what I'm hyped up to be," I added.

She nodded and went on.

"But you and I know each other without any of that baggage."

"Sure, I left it all in my room in London," I said, wittily.

She gave me a quick smile, to acknowledge my humor without encouraging it. Then she finished her thought.

"Michael, what we are now, is what we are."

I took Lisa's hand. Christ, she was so far ahead of me in understanding life. But I sure as hell understood how I felt about her.

"Lisa, I love you now."

She looked at me. Her eyes were more beautiful and knowledgeable than ever.

"I love you, too, Michael," she said. "Can it always be now?"

To myself I ordered: Don't let her get away again. Ever.

"Always," I pledged.

Chapter

16

I HAVE tried to think what I would have done differently if I had known how it was to come out.

As far as that particular time in Paris, I can't think of anything. For sure there were other times when better planning was definitely needed—but no changes on Paris. Even my French was improving.

Why it improved is beyond me. I mean, we spent something like seventy percent of the time in our room. (On one of our rare forays out, Madame Concierge asked if we had *mal de stomach* or something, while her husband was giving her little nudges with his elbow.) I did try to speak French when we went out to eat, or with Parisians along the Seine, so maybe that helped. Or maybe, well, Lisa did speak French—no, that's impossible. You really can't learn a foreign language by osmosis.

Anyway, I decided we needed to go farther than a few blocks away from the hotel.

"Lisa, we should go out."

"We were out this morning for an hour," she murmured from under the sheets beside me.

"No, 'out' out."

"You Americans are so restless," she said, tracing the letters of "Lisa + Michael" on my back.

"Shouldn't you at least call Claude and let her know we're back?"

I was losing my resolve for outside activity.

"Yes, I really should," she agreed, "in a while."

When she got to the letter "e" I turned over.

"How about in two hours as a kind of time frame?" I suggested, smiling.

Lisa sat up.

"You and your quickies," she pouted.

Three hours later, Lisa ventured downstairs to call Claude. When she returned, she went around the room throwing my clothes at me.

"Okay, turkey, we're going out," she announced.

"Wait," I protested. "I only said you should call."

"Claude says if we come over, she'll throw a little dinner together to celebrate our return."

Two things came out of our evening with Claude. One was Claude promised to teach Lisa and me some of her recipes and cooking techniques. The other was seeing the artwork on her walls gave me the urge to do some drawing. I was talking about my art talent when we got back to our room. Lisa picked up on it.

"You ever still draw, Michael?"

"Doodles, mostly," I replied.

"You just need a good model," Lisa said and recalling the afternoon in Chateauneuf when she sketched me, added, "Besides, it's my turn to pose."

I scrounged up some paper and a pencil from the concierge (she thought I wanted it to write letters) and started doing some sketches. Lisa was modeling nude, not really posing, but kind of relaxed on the bed with her head on one hand. The nice thing was I hadn't lost my drawing ability. I got a pretty good likeness going after a few tries. Even nicer than that was being able to study Lisa.

I mean, that's the thing about drawing. Okay, I know this sounds like artist's B.S., but you really do find out about what you draw. Now I knew her, her shapes and her forms, her lines and her curves.

We made love and I put to use all I had learned in drawing her.

"You like the drawings?" I asked.

"You know, Michael, you're really talented."

I thought a moment.

"A few minutes ago, Lisa, I was pretty impressed by your talents, too."

I'm certain since Lisa couldn't come up with an even halfway clever retort, she decided to turn to violence. She took a pillow and slammed me with it. Now standard dorm rules indicated I should reply in kind. I grabbed a pillow, but you can't trust those foreigners.

She tackled me while I was going into my windup.

We rolled around in the sheets, and I was about to reassert my superiority when I miscalculated the edge of the bed and landed on the floor.

"I always knew you'd leave me," Lisa said, looking down on my body.

She slid off the bed and crawled into my arms. We lay there together on the carpet, holding each other and saying nothing.

But I was thinking.

Would she like living in Los Angeles? Would I still?

Okay, so we'll live in Paris. Could I get into French films? I could get into painting, too. That's an idea. But would I look ridiculous in a beret?

Lisa's concerns were more immediate.

"What time is it?"

This necessitated a move over to the table for my watch.

"Eleven o'clock," I said.

"Only eleven?"

God! What was she thinking?

"Hey, take it easy—I've already broken several records," I reminded her.

"I'll call Guinness in the morning," she said. "Right now I have an idea."

Okay, so I'm curious.

"What?"

"Let's go to the Lido," she said enthusiastically.

Wait a minute. Lisa wanting to see a fancy floorshow? Could she be a closet bourgeois?

"Lisa, don't tell me you want to indulge in capitalist decadence?"

"Actually," said Lisa Foster, student, as she reached for her jeans, "I've always felt capitalist decadence was a lot more fun than the socialist kind."

In fifteen minutes we were in a cab heading for the Champs Élysées.

Everything was lit up and filled with people. The driver let us off and we looked around at the bright lights and stores, and then we went into the Lido.

Naturally, I wanted to get us a high-priced table. Lisa wouldn't go that far, so we ended up sitting at the bar. It was much more reasonable. And a lot easier on Lisa's conscience.

But the truth is, she loved it.

"I thought you don't like extravagance, Lisa."

"This is different, Michael. It's supposed to be extravagant."

It was that. In fact, I must say the whole show was astounding. Lots of leggy European girls dancing about. (Lisa wasn't too sure about me seeing that part; she didn't have to worry.) They even staged a medieval joust on stage.

Excellent!

Between acts Lisa got into a conversation with some guys and gals who were heading for Club 78, a wild place owned by a Brazilian. It was close by, but no way could we have made it in on our own—who knew me in Paris? The people we met took care of that.

Once inside, we danced like crazy to American and French and Brazilian music. Very jet-set. Very fancy. And jeans and all, Lisa looked great with her long legs going and her hair shaking in the lights. She only took a break to see if I was right about Rudolf Nureyev being there. He had shown up with a half-dozen dancers from his troupe.

Finally, Lisa and I both gave each other the "let's get outta here" sign. We happened to leave with the same crew we came in with. Just as everyone hit the street, all these flashbulbs went off in our faces. It was *paparazzi,* celeb photographers.

"Le fils!" they shouted.

It turned out our "friends" included the son of the president of France. Not too shabby a crowd. But you know what? It didn't bug me a bit the picture taking wasn't for me.

We said goodbye to *le fils* and associates and they headed off to their limos while Lisa and I walked up to an all-night cafe on the Champs Élysées. There we scarfed down some great chocolate éclairs. Yes, we decided the Lido, Club 78, the éclairs had all been astounding.

About four in the morning, Lisa and I got back to the room. I don't know when we fell asleep, but it was way past dawn.

I guess you might say we were pretty astounding ourselves.

Chapter

17

"WE can't go on living in a hotel together," I declared solemnly.

Lisa looked in apprehensively from the bathroom, where she was washing her hair.

"I suppose you're right," she agreed resignedly.

"Lisa, we'll just have to get an apartment."

She ran across the room and jumped on me. Her hair was wet and freezing cold against my skin.

"Okay, roomie," she whispered.

All this was the outcome of hours of internal debate with myself. It mainly had to do with my deciding that since I intended to stay in Paris with Lisa we had to get some kind of reality into our lives. Besides, the idea of living with Lisa (as opposed to sharing a hotel room) turned me on—you know, cooking, doing dishes, watching TV. Watching TV? Obviously, I really did have to learn French.

Also there was an added benefit to my living with Lisa. She would get used to living with me.

"Really, Michael, do you have to exercise an hour every morning?"

"Us stars"—breathe in—"have to"—breathe out—"stay in"—breathe in—"shape"—breathe out, collapse.

What we found was a one-bedroom two flights up, on the Rue Dauphine. The apartment brought even more reality: I had to start getting money out of my account in Los Angeles. That turned out to be less complicated than the rigmarole I went through to get the Churchill to ship my clothes from my abandoned hotel room. Anyway, we were together, on the Left Bank, cooking, doing dishes, and discussing whether to get a TV. "Okay, Lisa, so French TV isn't any better than American TV, it'd still help me learn the language." Did I mention grocery shopping? An event. Together we would go to shop after shop. The French are very specialized. The baker's. The butcher's. Meat shops for salami and prepared meats. The dairy. The fish market. Fruits and vegetables. And being human, every grocer got to be crazy about Lisa. After a few weeks they would put aside the pick of the day for our arrival.

Lisa was putting in a lot of hours with class and study, so I tried to take over the cooking. Let us say, charitably, that we ended up splitting it. She cooked and I ate. No, that's a joke, fans. I did a lot. But she was better at cooking, though. Lisa said that was definitely a legacy from her mother. I chipped in with my choicest recipes gleaned from years of bachelor living. And naturally, our kitchen was always open to Claude, when she felt like conducting gourmet classes. But no way were we bound to eat in every night. Not in Paris. Café Procope was right nearby, and there were lots more beyond. Without even counting the sidewalk crêpe stands for snacking (Lisa loved apricot crêpes).

While Lisa concentrated on her studies and the last days of Thomer's campaign, I started taking French lessons from one of Lisa's Canadian friends—Guy

Barrault. I also discovered the Café des Deux Magots, which is just across from the Church of St. Germain-des-Prés. Did I say I discovered it? It's only where Hemingway and all those expatriate writers used to hang out in the twenties. Lisa also took me to the Brassierie Lipp across the street, for talks about politics with her friends—and the possibility of running into some film people.

"Listen, Lisa, I really am not interested in running into film people."

"Are you kidding, Michael? You are a film person."

"Right now I'm a Lisa person."

"Hey, I don't want you to stop your career just because we enjoy making love."

"Okay, I'll think about it."

"Good," she said, smiling. "Now let's go do what we enjoy."

French cinema wasn't exactly waiting for Michael Shymkus. Not yet, anyway.

"I can't just call up Truffaut and say hi or *bonjour* or whatever," I told Lisa. She was in the kitchen making a salad and trying to read about Clemenceau and the First World War.

"Slice some bread for us, will you, hon?" she said.

"On the other hand, when my film comes out I'm in a much better position," I asserted.

"For what?" she asked, absent-mindedly.

"Are you listening to me?"

"Yes. You don't want to start pushing about acting in France until you see what's happening with your film in the U.S. so you can see whether you've got more clout. Is that it, Michael?"

"More or less."

"Fuck it, Michael, why don't you give Ron Peters a call and see what's going on?" she asked.

"I suppose I could. But that kind of gets me involved."

"You're not?" She had come in while I was setting the table.

"Hell, no. And I don't want to be," I insisted, trying to cover up my curiosity. "If it's big, I'll read about it in the *Herald.*"

"But, Michael, what if . . ." She considered whether to finish the question before going ahead. "What if it needs a little help?"

"You mean publicity?"

"That was the arrangement, wasn't it?"

"Lisa, you don't really believe all that crap about media hype—the picture goes on its own." I didn't really believe what I'd just said. But I was maybe half right. I mean, you couldn't prop up a bad picture with hype. But then, a little promotion could only help a good picture, right?

I was watching a TV talk show and having fruit and cheese and coffee. Lisa looked over from her reading and brought the subject up again.

"Do you think Peters would have you go on the *Tonight* show?" she asked me. "That's where all the big stars plug their movies, don't they?"

I said nothing. Who gave a shit about being on the *Tonight* show? That's just more hype. I shrugged and returned to the Brie, the coffee, and trying to figure out what the hell they were saying on TV. Actually, I had this little phrase book, which was next to no help. I looked at Lisa. She was wearing this floor-length yellow terry-cloth robe. And obviously, she was still interested in the Hollywood publicity machine.

"Imagine," Lisa went on, putting her history book on her lap, "pictures for fan magazines, articles in the leading newspaper, guest shots on variety shows."

I answered her in my W. C. Fields imitation:

"Ah, yes. The glamour of it all," I said, and added in my regular voice, "And little towns, eating by myself, missing planes, and late-night talk shows back to back with sunrise talk shows."

"You still miss it, Michael?"

"Nowhere near as much as I would miss you, Lisa."

"Goddammit," she said, not pissed but in a matter-of-fact way. "I can't carry it, Michael. You're a film actor. It's what you do."

"It's more complicated than that," I said, racing my brain for a solution to this conversation. "Or is it?"

Lisa looked at me, figuring out what I was thinking even as I was thinking it.

"Oh, no, you don't, Mike, I've already decided I don't fit in there."

"Eve was the one who was worried—and she ain't in it no more," I reminded Lisa. "Besides, have you ever been to the United States?"

"I was in Buffalo once," Lisa said. "Does that count?"

I started looking through the drawers of our desk for my address book.

"I can call Ron Peters in the morning," I said, pushing papers aside. "You'll be swimming at the Beverly Hills Hotel pool in a week."

"In a week?" she said, and I sensed the concern in her voice.

"Oh, Jesus," I said, stopping my address search, "you've got the campaign."

"I suppose school's not that important, either," she said, closing her book.

"That's it! Everything we do is important," I declared. "We'll go when your classes are finished. The election's over by then, too. And we'll be back in Paris by the fall."

"I can see it now," Lisa said, waving her hand across an imaginary headline. "Actor Michael Shymkus and his girlfriend fly in from Europe for premiere!"

"Girlfriend?" I repeated. "The actor and his girlfriend—sounds like sleaze city from here."

"You prefer 'concubine'?" She grinned.

"I prefer 'bride.' "

The idea just kind of popped out like that, maybe because it had been sitting inside me a long time.

"Are you sure you're saying what I think you're saying?"

"Only if you think I'm saying marriage," I said.

She touched her lips.

"Michael, I'm just learning how to be a roommate," she said. "I don't know diddly-squat about being a wife."

"Lisa, will you marry me?"

"Well, if you put it that way," she said, looking straight at me with her beautiful eyes, "yes."

"Yes?" I wondered.

"Yes," she said. "If it's what you want?"

"Yes," I affirmed.

"Then it's yes," she said.

"Yes," I said.

That night I woke to find Lisa sitting up.

"Wassamatter?" I asked.

"Well, what if I meet Burt Reynolds at a Hollywood cocktail party and he makes some lewd suggestion to me?" she speculated. "What should I say, you know, me being a married woman and all?"

"Tell him to fuck off."

"I'll tell him, 'My husband says for you to fuck off.' "

She lay back down, but I could sense her laughing to herself.

I know this is ridiculous, but I spent the rest of the night trying to figure out how I was going to handle Burt Reynolds. Goddammit to hell! He would go after Lisa. Good thing I decided to marry her *before* we leave for L.A.

Chapter

18

Dear Mom and Dad,

Good talking with you the other night. Lisa is excited about meeting you. I know you'll be crazy about her. Bet you thought I would be single forever. Did I tell you Notre Dame cathedral is an easy walk from the apartment. Okay, write me at 10, Rue Dauphine, Paris 6ᵉ, France.

love,

Michael

P.S. Lisa sends her love.

Napoleon's invasion of Russia must have entailed less planning than our wedding.

I mean, for what we had decided not to make into a big deal (the actual wedding, not the idea of marrying Lisa—that was a *big deal*), there were seemingly a number of details to be dealt with.

169

Even no fuss required fussing.

My big contribution to the general confusion was to invite my parents and my brother to come to Paris. My dad had been to Europe as a peacetime soldier stationed in Germany, my mother, never. Same for little brother. This was the single touchiest part for me—my parents. Lisa never said anything, but I was always aware her parents were not around to see their daughter's marriage. As much as possible, I wanted mine to be hers and all that. Yet, hell, Claude was stepping right in as mother of the bride.

It was Claude who organized the shower.

I suppose I could say we only went along with the kitchen shower just to be polite to Lisa's friends at La Maison Canadienne, but the fact was Lisa was really touched. And for the record, so was I.

"This will keep us happy for a while, Michael," said Lisa while showing off the prize of the loot: a box filled with index cards on which each of the girls had written their favorite recipe *en français*.

"I'm looking under H for hamburger," said I, flipping through the recipe cards—unreadable to me—and going on to some of the other gadgetry. There were a set of wooden spoons, a timer, and a pair of Eiffel Tower salt and pepper shakers—there's always a joker. And some other paraphernalia, besides.

We were in our living room (it was the dining room during dinner hours) with the gadgets spread on the floor. "Little Mikey" had taken up residence on top of the TV. I began to wonder if when we had our kid would I go the junior route in naming. Mikey—the kid will probably think he was named after a toy lion. Or would she be Michaela. We could still say little Mikey.

Lisa took out some stationery.

"I'll drop Eve a note," she said, starting to write.

Am I a vindictive person? Of course not. It's just it

was supposed to be a small wedding. That meant my parents, Claude Saché, and a few of Lisa's friends. Oh, and my brother Gary as best man.

"I'll make a deal with you," I countered.

"A deal? I see you're getting ready for your return to Hollywood."

"When we get to L.A. we'll leave a message on Eve's answering service," I said. "Lisa and Michael called. We're married. Up yours."

Lisa put the paper away.

"I'll try again when you come up with something less tacky," she said.

Sunday we made the trek out to Versailles, to see how the Sun King, Louis XIV, lived. Better than we, definitely. We went through the main building, and Lisa filled me in on what it was like. In the Hall of Mirrors, I flashed on the royalty that was once there—it must have seemed it would last forever, and nothing does. Then, out into the gardens. The gardens are really like a forest. We wandered among the trees for a good two hours. Our big discovery was a carousel tucked in a clearing in the trees. Here we are at what has got to be the most spectacular palace in the world and we're turned on by a carousel. There were children riding it. Lisa and I took a spin, too.

The next day while Lisa was in class I hit a couple of museums on my own: The Modern Art, or as they say, Art Moderne, and the Musée de Cinéma. When I got back Lisa was already home.

"You're not going to believe this," she said, her eyes so bright a green they crowded out the blue. "Look!"

She handed me a registered envelope. I knew the return address from the design. It was Peters Productions.

"I wonder why they never can wait for me to call them."

"Yeah, Michael, it's not like you were hiding out or something," Lisa snickered.

"I *was* going to call them."

I sat down at the table to read the letter. There was some general crap, "Trust you are enjoying yourself in Paris," and an aside on what I was really most curious about: How the hell did they get my address? I mean, who blew my cover? It wasn't the Crocker National Bank (three cheers for them) or even O'Connor, who had shipped all my stuff from my apartment. Instead, it was my own mother. Well, she had always warned me, "Son, don't trust anyone, not even your own mother . . . especially your own mother." Actually, I had never told her not to hand out my address, thinking no one would ask my folks—a definite oversight.

But let's get right to it, that was not all I was searching for in the letter. In fact, I didn't have to search at all. It was right there in plain English so the fugitive could understand. I was to come to Los Angeles within ten days to start publicity or be held in breach of contract. So much for not putting in a phone to avoid contact with tbe outside world.

"What's up, Michael?" Lisa asked.

"Just some legal crap," I said.

Lisa was not going to let me mope.

"C'mon," she inquired, "have they decided to reshoot the picture as a musical comedy?"

"Not exactly."

"They're mad because you wouldn't send them a wedding invitation?"

This wasn't going to be easy.

"Let's go over to Deux Magots," I said, suddenly wanting to get away from the place where we had been discovered.

"Okay, Michael."

It was still light outside. Lisa was wearing this

really neat gray western shirt that was trimmed in red. We made the walk without saying a word to each other. Lisa didn't ask and I didn't answer. At the Café des Deux Magots we sat down and I ordered a couple of bourbons and water, of all things. We didn't drink them anyway.

Lisa waited for me to let her in on the problem. I did.

"Ron says I have to get to L.A. or I won't get paid." She took the practical approach.

"Michael, we were going to make the trip in a few weeks anyway, right?"

"I guess so," I confirmed, although I had still hoped to get out of it.

"So what's the prob?" Lisa asked, her green eyes blinking once.

"I have to be there within ten days."

"Shit! The election's over, but I still have classes."

"That's the prob," I said.

I knew what her solution would be. I should go now and she would join me in June. Hell, it was the only one that made any sense—which is exactly why I was suspicious of it.

And I wasn't the only one.

"This isn't fair," Lisa said. "I mean, if we're going to spend our entire lives together why am I panicked over you being away from me for six weeks?"

We went over the thing again and again—maybe those assholes were only threatening a lawsuit. Probably the whole thing was just to scare me into coming. Besides, what the hell was a lawsuit, anyway. Plenty. Lisa said it wasn't worth risking all I had worked for just because of a six-week difference. I decided to be very noble. I said it was just as ridiculous for her to pull out of school right now. I was also hoping she wouldn't agree with me. The net was we would just have to tough it out apart until school was over. That was that. Oh, and I would fly back for the wedding.

Wait a minute. Fly back for the wedding? We hadn't even gotten to that part in any detail. I had some ideas on the subject.

"Lisa, I don't want to wait any more to get married."

"But it was always going to be when school's over."

"I wasn't always going to be leaving."

"What about your parents? Your brother? Our plans?"

"Screw all that."

"That's a bunch of shit."

"Huh?"

"Michael," she said solemnly, "things are screwed up enough."

That's the truth. Why the hell hadn't I told my mother not to give out my address?

Ridiculous as it sounds, for Lisa it was a kind of an issue of principle. It just really rubbed her wrong that we had to go and change all our plans around this trip. The fact was we loved each other and we were getting married. She felt we ought to be able to survive six weeks. Besides, Lisa reasoned, this is the way it would be in the future. Me going off to make some picture or public appearance. So we should just live with it. I countered I would always be able to take her with me. Anyway, I figured just the opposite about our present situation. Since we were getting married, what's to wait? So she can stand up to Hollywood? Not letting them push us around? Hell, didn't she love me now?

"I do love you now, Michael. But don't we want more than now?"

I was sorry I could have ever questioned her.

"Oh, look, Lisa, they got us fighting each other."

I reached out for her and we held one another tightly.

"Okay, Michael, if you want we can get a quickie wedding."

I guess I lied to be gallant, and let the moment get
away.

"I just wanted to know that," I said. "Let's wait and
do it right."

"You turkey," Lisa said, beaming, "you just better be
well rested when you get back."

We stayed at Thomer's home all the night of the
election. Lisa was everywhere, while I spent most of
my time trying to help Mrs. Thomer serve coffee and
pastries. Two days before the *préfet* of Paris had en-
dorsed Thomer but there had not been time to get that
news around. Still, by one in the morning we knew
Lisa's and all the others' work had paid off. It would be
Conseiller Thomer from now on. Lisa was very reserved and ladylike. She screamed her head off and
beat on an old African drum the Thomers had.

Chapter

19

IT was still dark when the buzzer went off on the alarm clock. I started to get dressed.

"Hey, Mr. Hollywood, do you have to run off in such a rush?" Lisa asked.

"Not if you're up," I answered.

She took my hand and pulled me to her.

"It's whether you're up that counts," she said and smiled.

Because of that unscheduled delay I canceled out on Lisa's plan to get us to the Porte Maillot terminal by Métro. Instead, we took a taxi. I was becoming goal-oriented again.

We went over the phone-call system once more. I would call every other night to La Maison Canadiénne. Meanwhile, if Lisa needed to reach me she should call Ron Peters Productions and tell them when and where to call her back. "Michael, it's silly to spend all this money. I'll write to you." We also decided she should go ahead and get reservations for my parents and brother at the George V—my dad would like that—for the week of our wedding. Lisa insisted I bring her clippings of some of the publicity and reviews about the movie. I told her there would be plenty of stuff left over for when we got back to the U.S. in June.

The cab driver put on the radio. A song by Edith Piaf was playing. It crossed my mind I could cry, but I pushed the thought away. From the car we saw too much. It was a real catalogue of Paris. We crossed the Seine and spotted Notre Dame. We drove past the Louvre. The Eiffel Tower. The Place de la Concorde and up the Champs Élysées. The Arc de Triomphe.

Lisa began to cry.

"I'm sorry, goddammit," she said without a trace of flipness. "I can't help it."

Instead of a limo or cab I took the airport bus out to De Gaulle airport from Porte Maillot. That was for Lisa; she couldn't seem to realize this trip was paid for. I will say Ron had been pretty decent about my travel. I had first-class reservations on an Air France 747. Also, I was landing in Chicago (actually, they do a quick stop first in Montreal—Lisa gave me the number of a cousin to call). After seeing my folks, I would go on to Los Angeles. So here I was: going back to L.A. to open my first big movie. I was a star—well, I could be a star—and all I'm wondering is, why the hell am I leaving Paris?

The plane got up and I put on the headset. In my mind I saw Lisa waving to me, tears on her cheek. I had told her not to worry; I would call as soon as I got in. I felt terrible inside, but I was determined to be calm. Over the headset came the same goddamn song we had heard the first night at La Méditerranée. That did it. I couldn't help the tears coming to my eyes. The businessman next to me started looking uncomfortable.

I took off the headset and went quietly back to the restroom. Inside I broke. I couldn't stop myself. I guess I really didn't want to.

I just stood there and bawled my damn head off at thirty thousand feet.

Chapter

20

TYPICAL Shymkus situation.

There I was staying at the Beverly Hills Hotel. My entire career was about to bust wide open and make me a STAR. And I'm wishing I were somewhere else.

As a point of fact, the movie looked fantastic. When I got into L.A. from Chicago—where, by the way, my parents were one thousand percent excited about my wedding—Ron Peters set up a screening for me. I took a pass on it for that night, but I caught it the next afternoon. It really came off great. To give you an idea of how much I liked it, I called Wesley Crouch to offer my congratulations. That's not to say there weren't any scenes where I would have used different takes. I knew I was better than in some of the selects they used. But, overall, I just didn't feel like quibbling. Not when it's that good. I mean, the word was getting around. "Hey, Michael, I heard your new flick is fantastic!"

Actually the whole trip should have been a ball. I'm back in L.A. I'm lying by the pool at the Beverly Hills Hotel. I'm meeting my old friends. I'm getting my picture taken for publicity stills. I'm being interviewed for magazine articles. But there was that one key element missing.

Lisa.

"I really miss you, Li—"

"You? What about the way I miss you, Michael?"

Okay, so our phone conversations were not laden with heavy meaning. We had been torn apart—that's what had happened—and the only thing that could help a little was the sound of each other's voice.

"I'm making a list of things we can do in L.A. when I bring you here," I said.

"I need something to look forward to," Lisa said. "I'm so lonely, I've taken to sleeping with little Mikey."

That toy lion was having all the fun.

"You're doing better than I am, Lisa."

"I'll bet."

"Hey, now, that hurts," I protested.

"Can I kiss it and make it well?"

Oh, God, I loved her so much those phone calls were pure torture. That's got to be the definition of frustration. Talking to Lisa and not being able to see her or touch her. Was it only for another four weeks? Forever!

There was a cocktail party at the Beverly Hilton for some magazine writers and some key theater owners. I went late on purpose—let 'em wait. What amazed me is the angle the writers were trying to develop about Paris. What was I doing there? Was it true? Had I fallen in love with a famous French actress? Or was she royalty? (No, assholes, she's Lisa—which makes her far superior to your goddamn handles) I just smiled and kept trying to move the conversation back to the film.

Ron came up to me and said I was doing terrific; the press was curious about me. He wanted to know what the deal was with Lisa. Would I bring her back with

me? Who would I introduce her as? (Try my wife for
starters.)

This was all small talk for Ron. What he really
wanted to find out was would I read the script for the
new feature. My half-baked plan revolved around living in Paris and maybe doing a couple of pictures a
year. The idea was to set it up so Lisa could come along
wherever I had to go. A lot of that depended on how
this film did. That is, whether I would have the clout to
make that kind of long-distance deal, or whether I
should be in L.A. hustling. Screw it, I couldn't worry
about that now. I asked Ron if he could have the script
sent to me at the Beverly Hills Hotel. He told me it
would be there when I got back.

The script was waiting. I went up to my room (when
Lisa comes I was determined to get one of the bunga-
lows) and put through a call to Paris. Lisa was not at
La Maison Canadienne, so I asked for Claude.

"Allo?"

"Claude, it's Michael."

"Oh, how is it there?"

"I miss Lisa, that's about all."

"She is very sad without you, Michael."

It was good to hear Claude's accent again. But I still
didn't know where Lisa was. She was supposed to be
there tonight.

"Was Lisa by earlier?"

"Nom de Dieu, I have not seen her since two days."

I was telling myself this meant nothing. Lisa was
busy with school or something. But that's bullshit, she
was supposed to be there tonight.

"Claude, can you ask one of Lisa's friends to stop by
the apartment?"

"Oui, yes, I will."

Claude wasn't all that worried. But I gave her the
number of the Beverly Hills Hotel and made her swear

to call me collect when she knew anything. The only thing for certain was I couldn't concentrate on reading any script.

The next day was kind of lost. I refused to leave the hotel for fear of missing any phone calls. The publicity people did set up an interview for me, anyway, What a bunch of leeches! They sent a writer over to do something with a Chicago angle—you know, home-town boy kind of crap—to get into the Chicago papers. Right after she left I called La Maison Canadienne.

"I want to talk to Claude—or Lisa Foster if she's there."

"Who is this?" asked the voice.

"Michael Shymkus."

"This is Sue Chalgrin," she said. I remembered her as one of Lisa's friends. "Claude is out and I haven't seen Lisa around anywhere."

Jesus, if the idea of the call was to make me feel better, it was a disaster. I gave my number to Sue. She promised to look around school for Lisa. After I hung up I tried real hard to watch television.

About an hour later the phone rang. I was literally shaking when I answered.

"Mr. Shymkus, this is the desk."

"Yes, is it collect? I accept."

"Sir, there's an Eve Ross here to see you. She's waiting in the Polo Lounge."

Hell! What was Eve showing up now for? I had purposely avoided her. I paged her in the Polo Lounge. There's nothing that bitch loves better than being paged in the Polo Lounge. Naturally, the phone would be brought to her table.

"Eve, I can't see you now," I said, without even saying hello. "I'm expecting a phone call."

"You can be paged right here, Michael. Try to be polite, will you?"

Eve was sitting by herself at the back of one of the big circular booths. The phone was in front of her.

"What do you want, Eve?" I asked, getting to the point.

"I was going to say Paris agrees with you, but it only seems to have made you ruder."

I told Eve again I was waiting for a phone call. I also told her I was not interested in talking with her for whatever reason. She ignored that and said the film was very hot, and therefore, so was I. Most people still thought of her and me together. She also reminded me it was I who had broken off our agreement.

I thanked her for the history lesson and gave her the news.

"I'm marrying Lisa."

Eve said nothing. Written all over her face was, "Why now?" Even Eve Ross couldn't make Lisa Foster Shymkus into a "media person." No all-night dancing at Regine's and whatever other spot is chic that week. No pool parties in Bel Air. Why, we had to crash Club 78. Lisa was not part of the "scene."

In other words, Lisa was no help to my Career.

"What are you looking for, Michael—a house, kids, the whole ball of wax?" Eve asked me.

"You got it, baby."

"Well, Michael," she said, "you can always fall back on talent."

Eve smiled. So did I.

"Michael Shymkus. Paging Michael Shymkus."

I picked up the phone that was sitting between Eve and me.

"Michael Shymkus?"

"Yes."

I heard the operator say, "Go ahead, Paris."

What the hell was this? I had told Lisa to call collect.

"Lisa, is that you?"

"Michael, this is Claude."

"Where's Lisa?"

"She is in the hospital."

"No."

"She has accident. Very bad."

Oh, Jesus God. I knew I should have never gone away. Claude was not doing such a good job of holding herself together, either. She didn't take to English easily under relaxed circumstances. She was barely making sense now. I got that there was an accident. Lisa had been crossing a street and was hit by a car. There had already been some surgery.

The only thing that was getting to me was why the fuck was I sitting in Los Angeles when I should be in Paris?

"We're getting married." I restated that out loud to myself and Eve and to the world which seemed to be working overtime to screw up our lives. I was trying to control myself and not doing it. I did tell Eve to tell Ron I would call him when I knew more. Then I ran out. The rest of the night was spent trying to find out the first flight I could make to Paris. There was no sleep, that was for sure. Just let Lisa be alive, I prayed, and I'll never leave her again.

Oh, God, let her live.

Chapter

21

I PROBABLY should have shaved or rested or something, but I didn't. I went straight to Val de Grâce hospital.

There had been plenty of time on the flight over to worry about every possibility. The one that kept coming up, and I kept pushing back, was not making it in time. I would not allow myself to name in time for what. That was a given. But then, Claude hadn't talked about there being that much danger. I guess I've just got a low opinion of hospitals. You know, like that's the end. Which is really dumb on my part. I mean, hospitals are to help people. I really should have gone when I was sick in London. Would it make any difference to have Dr. Poole come to Paris? They must have doctors in France—they have hospitals. Just let Lisa out of this, God. That is all I ask.

The sister showed me to Lisa's room. She went in first and announced me. I heard a weak response. But it was still Lisa.

At least the voice was Lisa's. The biggest difference was a cast the entire length of her left leg. And the wire holding it to the metal supports for traction. And the bandage on her cheek and her forehead.

"Can't I get any privacy around here?" Lisa quipped, softly.

"Oh, Lisa," was all I could say.

"Wait until Halloween," she whispered. "I can go as a mummy." There was probably a topper to that line, but I didn't try it. What I did was walk over and take her free hand. She was getting intravenous in the other arm.

"You'll do anything to get my attention," I said, trying to keep it light.

"The thing that really pisses me off is it was my fault."

"Come on, Lisa."

"No, really. I was walking across the street to mail you a letter—I'm too cheap to call—and I was busy daydreaming when the car hit me."

"Do I at least get to see the letter?"

"Who knows where it is now?" she said. "I'll tell you one thing—from now on I phone ahead."

I looked at her eyes. They were as beautiful as ever. More so to me, seeing her alive.

"Goddamn French drivers," I said.

"Watch it, Michael, the place is full of nuns."

I closed the door a little more.

"Where else are you hurt?" I asked.

"Not there, if that's what you're worried about."

"For Christ's sakes, Lisa, I wasn't thinking about that," I insisted, shaking my head. "I mean, we should at least wait until you're off IV."

Suddenly her eyes winced in pain. She tightened her hand on mine. Nothing was said until she relaxed.

"It's okay now," she said.

"Yeah, sure. Quit shittin' me, Lisa."

"It was terrible, Michael. It didn't even hurt at

first—but later, I thought I was going to die from pain."

I felt fear inside me. I said something to counteract it.

"You're going to be okay," I said, wanting so badly to say something comforting. "It hurts now but you're going to be okay."

"I didn't realize how bad it was until I saw me in the stainless steel in the emergency room—what I looked like. It couldn't be me. I started screaming."

"Always looks worse," I said, and realized there was nothing I could say that sounded right.

The sister came in with a hypo to kill the pain. She asked me to step out.

During the next morning I figured out I had been something like forty-four hours without sleep. I guess somehow I thought I could split the pain with Lisa and make it less. Finally, Claude came to the room. She ordered me to get some rest.

It was hard enough going into our apartment. In fact, I couldn't get myself into our bed. I slept on the couch until three that afternoon. When I went back to the hospital I got little Mikey out of our bed and took it with me.

Lisa was sleeping when I got there. There would be a lot of that. I put the toy lion next to her. What I wanted to work out was to make sure somebody, Claude or myself, would always be there when Lisa woke up.

Claude was sitting beside her. As it turned out, she didn't have much more to add to what Lisa had told me. Just that it was raining when it happened and the guy couldn't stop. It was an older car, a Simca. The police were lifting his license, but beyond that—well, it was an accident. An accident. Jesus! The large bone of the leg was completely fractured. Ribs were cracked. There were internal injuries too, but she didn't know exactly what. Lisa had taken blood transfusions. I made a promise to myself, which I kept, to give some blood to help replace it. There were facial cuts, too.

Since Lisa was still sleeping, and Claude was there, I went to the lobby and made a call to Ron Peters in L.A.

His secretary put me right through.

"Michael, I'm really sorry," he said.

"At least she's alive."

I heard Ron ask some people to wait outside. Jesus, this was the royal treatment. Getting through to Ron, and now a private phone call.

"What's the extent of the injuries?" he asked.

I was amazed. I mean, hell, Ron was being halfway decent about the whole thing. I knew damn well what he wanted to know was when I'd be coming to L.A., but he'd be damned if he'd come out and ask that. Let's face it, he'd be within his rights to wonder—there was several million bucks involved. That's his job. I mean, he's trying to open a movie and I'm trying to hold on to what's left of my screwed-up life.

"I really don't know for sure; broken leg, some kind of internal injuries; they've got her pretty doped up for pain," I said, not wanting to get into a lot of detail long-distance.

"You getting any sleep?"

"I'm not too tired right now," I answered, thinking how much I ached.

"Don't get all worn out, Michael."

Oh, okay. I'll bring it up.

"I suppose you're interested in how long I'll be here," I said, getting around to the big subject.

"Sure I am," Ron admitted. "But you don't have to deal with that right now."

Not deal with, maybe. Worry about, yes. But it was a cinch I couldn't do shit about anything. Lisa's condition was out of my hands, and yet it made a difference being with her. Ron could understand that. At least he seemed to.

"Michael, will you let me know if I can do anything?"

Right, where should I start? Might as well get into it now.

"Ron, I'd like some advances on money—this is going to be pretty expensive."

"It's tight, Michael, opening a new picture and all," he informed me. "We'll talk about it when you get back."

Who said anything about coming back?

"Ron, I'm not sure—"

"Listen, keep me posted, and don't hesitate to call."

So much for that phone call.

The money problem had been tumbling around in my head. Costs were starting to pile up. There was my travel, rent, phone calls, doctor bills—and I had zip coming in. And besides, what if Lisa needed more surgery? Let's face it, my cash reserves were starting to stretch thin. I also had the feeling when Peters had heard Lisa was still alive, he figured I should rush right back. No, hell, he had been pretty nice. Now it was just a matter of squeezing more money out of him. A bit tacky, this money issue. Especially since I was in breach of contract again. One thing was for sure: I had done a shit job negotiating. Well, I would just have to pull together some figures and lay a number on him. He didn't sound too thrilled about the subject, though.

I ambled back to the room. On either side I caught quick shots of people stuck in the hospital. It did nothing to make me feel any less down.

Lisa was still asleep. Claude met me at the door. She was going back to La Maison Canadienne. My watch now. Claude looked tired, and I realized how she had stuck by Lisa from the moment she first heard. Yes, but at the beginning, Lisa was by herself. All the goddamn time I was sitting in Los Angeles, I should have been with Lisa.

The only thing to do was to sit down and wait for Lisa to come around. I could see the black-and-blue marks on the inside of her elbow where they took blood samples. Her skin really looked pale to me. What I couldn't see was her face. The guy must have swerved his car, though. Her arms were okay—no breaks. I laughed wryly to myself. Right, no bad breaks.

God, what *would* all this cost? It's Europe, so they've got to have some kind of medical deal. Only Lisa isn't a French citizen, so she isn't covered. Maybe she was done with the worst of it. But who knew? I mean, what the hell are internal injuries?

And what about our wedding?

One thing was for sure; I was through putting off the wedding. I decided if we had married before I left this would have never happened; as if one thing had anything to do with the other. So that's the move. Put together a whole wedding right here in the hospital.

I could go around and get all the permits or whatever the hell you need. We'd invite the staff and Lisa's doctors. With all this my parents couldn't come, but they would understand. I mean, there was no sense in the world in letting a foreign car tell me I should put off my wedding. Besides, Lisa could be laid up for weeks, right?

"Sister, do you speak English? I need some information."

"I speak a little."

"How long do you think Lisa will be like this?"

"She is seriously injured."

"A week?"

"I cannot say."

"Two weeks?"

"You must ask the doctor."

By the next afternoon, I had gotten myself all hepped up on the prospect of the hospital wedding. What a coup. I hadn't said a word when I thought of it. Now just wait until Lisa came around and I laid the idea on her. I wondered if they'd have to change her name on all her records.

Lisa's eyes opened. The lids kind of fluttered and then she looked at the ceiling for a long time. Here I was looking at this pale girl with beautiful eyes and soft hair.

"Good morning," I said.

"It's morning?" asked the still hazy patient.

"Figure of speech. Actually it's two in the afternoon," I said, realizing it didn't really matter what the hell time it was. But you need those kind of reference points.

She turned her head to me.

"I think I'm late for class."

I started pacing off the floor.

"What are you doing?" she asked.

"I'm measuring the room," I replied.

"Is somebody else coming in?" Lisa wondered, starting to be more fully awake.

"We'll try to keep the number small," I muttered. "That means offending some people. . . ."

She was awake now.

"Did the sister slip you a shot or something?" she asked. (Actually, they did give me some *nitrate de bismuth* for nervous stomach.)

"Lisa, I'm trying to plan our wedding," I went on, double-checking the width of the room.

"Yes," I said, "this room will do very nicely."

"Oh, Michael," Lisa said, and turned her head back so she was looking at the ceiling again.

"Hey, your enthusiasm is underwhelming," I observed.

"The bride wore a veil of white bandages," she said, "That really sucks."

"Now you're being really superficial," I said, to get our priorities in order. "So cut the shit, okay?"

"First of all, you don't know shit from Shinola," she said, "and second of all, you don't know what's under all this plaster and bandages."

"You," I said. "Or somebody doing a good imitation."

She looked at me again, but she didn't speak. Not at first. She seemed to be taking time—time to let me get on to what she was going to say.

"I need to have an operation, Michael."

"I thought you were on the mend," I said, sounding more suspicious than I meant to.

Lisa filled me in on the whole story. When the car hit her there were the fractured bones and cracked ribs. The doctor had given her a detailed list of the damage. There was no way I could listen to this and not cringe—Lisa wouldn't hold that against me. Her face was cut and her cheekbone or malar was fractured. They had to check the facial nerve and make sure the parotid duct was intact. It was, but I didn't ask whatever the hell that is. They then did some surgery to pack the cheek and put the skin back, sew up other cuts, and get her broken leg set. The cracked ribs should heal themselves. But what about the internal injuries? Now there seemed to be malfunctioning of the spleen which was affecting her blood and the ability to fight infection. Not good.

"Michael, I don't know if I'm going to be right again for a long time—maybe never."

I reached out and took Lisa's hand. I held it very tightly.

"I'd like a little more credit than that, Lisa," I said. "You can't get rid of me that easy."

I felt Lisa try to squeeze my hand. Barely.

"Good," she said. "Then we can wait and do it on our time."

"But why?" I asked. "Nothing's going to change the way I feel."

"You mean that, don't you?" she said.

I sat there with my hospital wedding plans on the brink of folding up. Lisa spoke again.

"I just don't want any charity, Michael," she continued.

"Good. Okay, no charity. Now will you marry me?" I asked.

"Yes."

We sat there and said nothing. It was for sure. Then I tried, in my bumbling way, to change the subject.

"You know, the French are supposed to be terrific surgeons," I said.

"And shitty drivers," Lisa came back, topping my line.

"No, really—" I started.

The sister came in and changed the IV bottle.

Lisa moved her arm to make things easier for the sister.

"I hope there's a little more pepper in it this time," Lisa said.

"Yes, and is the vintage agreeable to your sensitive palate?" I inquired, picking up on her bit.

The sister looked at both of us strangely. Lisa translated the whole thing into French for her. We got a smile out of the nun. Not much of one, though. The sister gave her a hypo.

Lisa turned to me, sighing.

"This is a tough crowd, Michael."

"Hell," I said, "wait'll we give them the A material."

"That reminds me," she said, "you haven't told me anything about your trip to Hollywood."

"Strictly the pits."

"Besides that."

I started on the story of the cocktail party at the Beverly Hilton.

My fiancée fell asleep.

Chapter

22

AT first I decided not to call my folks, thinking their feelings would be hurt if they couldn't be at the wedding. Then I changed my head around and not only called them, I also called my brother, two high school friends, and Bob O'Connor. On my side, that's as close to a big social occasion as it got. Except that O'Connor wanted to fly in. I talked him out of it. He finally agreed, saying I would need a bachelor party a lot more after I'd been married for a while.

The wedding arrangements actually only took four days to make. I mean, a day and a half for me to give up on the French bureaucracy, and the rest of the time for Claude to get everything set. (I did get the rings—Florentine gold.) Fortunately, I had filed an initial request for when we had originally scheduled our wedding, so that paperwork was started. But the biggest problem was getting a civil ceremony. See, here we were in this hospital with all these nuns and priests and everything and we wanted to keep it all nice and unreligious. That meant we had to go to the *arrondissement,* which is like a city ward, and get the mayor of the *arrondissement,* who is really only like an alderman, to come over to the hospital. Conseiller Thomer was a big help there.

Claude wore a new dress for the ceremony. I put on a suit. Oh, and even though no one would see it, I got the car washed. There really wasn't any way for Lisa to make an entrance, so we kind of waited in the hall until Claude said we could come in. Lisa's doctor, Dr. Gautier, was there, and so were two of the sisters. Naturally, Conseiller Thomer showed, much to the mayor's pleasure. We had finally gotten the crew from La Maison Canadienne cut to three: Rosalind Bradley, Alex Chevron, and Francine Sommerand—who brought her guitar. (I was very down on the guitar bit, but it really turned out to be a nice thing.)

Claude opened the door for us. I had ordered flowers for the room. It looked pretty nice, considering. And despite everything, Lisa looked beautiful. Absolutely unequivocally, no excuses beautiful. Her energy was also up for this—no small task, given her condition. She even had me stick a rose in the foot part of her cast.

The only thing that bugged me was the mayor—Monsieur Capet—insisted on bringing a photographer. He figured performing a ceremony in a hospital ought to be worth a publicity shot in the paper. Lisa took his side on this, so we posed for a couple of pictures. Thomer included, of course, and then threw the photog out.

By this time, Dr. Gautier was giving me signs to get things over with. The biggest concern was Claude, who totally lost her cool. She started crying and going on in French and holding Lisa's hand. One of the sisters had to go out and get her some water to settle her down.

think Dr. Gautier threw a little something extra in it, besides.

Finally, we got everyone organized. I walked over and took Lisa's hand. Monsieur Capet, who wasn't any taller than the bedpost, started going through the service in French. Just after he seemed to get warmed up, he stopped and nodded to me.

I figured this was my cue, so I said, "I do."

"You're supposed to say *oui*," Lisa told me.

But how do you say 'I do' in French?" I asked, humbly.

"You don't say 'I do,' you say *oui*," she insisted.

I leaned over and whispered to Lisa out of the side of my mouth.

"Are you sure this is legal?" I wanted to know.

"Just try to get out of it," Lisa replied.

Everyone was waiting through this exchange. I nodded understanding of my position to Lisa and turned to the people.

"*Oui*," I said.

Monsieur Capet looked relieved. He didn't speak a word of English, so God knows what he thought we were discussing.

He went on again for a while. Soon it was my turn. This time I didn't need any coaching.

"*Oui*," I said.

He said a few more words and stopped and smiled. Alex Clarke gave me the rings. I put Lisa's on her finger and she did the same for me. Monsieur Capet finished up. He looked at me expectantly.

I turned to Lisa for counsel. She was smiling.

"We're married," she said. "How about a kiss?" As I started to kiss Lisa, Dr. Gautier warned me to be careful because of her injured cheekbone, so I only gave her a little kiss. I still didn't feel complete so I leaned forward and whispered in her ear:

"I love you, Lisa."

"And I love you, Michael, until you-know-when—an
beyond," Lisa whispered back.

I straightened up and faced everyone. Monsieur Cape
gave me a big grin and kissed me on both cheeks. S
did Dr. Gautier and Claude, who was still blubbering
Thomer came up with two bottles of champagne. We
had about ten minutes of this when Sister Geneviève
started getting worried about everything being too
much for Lisa. We quieted down, but Lisa still wanted
Francine to play a couple of songs for us on her guitar.
Francine sang softly in French while we finished our
champagne. Before she finished Lisa had fallen asleep.

I saw everyone down the hall and returned to the
room. I took Lisa's hand and sat down beside her.

Sometime in the night I opened my eyes to find Lisa
looking at me.

"I know you," she said. "You're Lisa's husband."

I nodded at my new identity.

"Can I kiss you, Mrs. Shymkus?" I requested.

"Very carefully," she instructed me.

Really, all I did was kind of brush her lips.

"How's that?" I asked.

"I knew you only married me for sex."

She squeezed my hand and I saw her close her eyes. I
settled back in my chair.

"Hey, Li, I do hope you're giving me a rain check on
the honeymoon?"

"I don't know, Michael," she replied. "This is the best
one I've ever had."

Chapter

23

AFTER all we had gone through to get set up in Paris, we found ourselves talking about Los Angeles. Lisa was more curious than ever about the "scene." She let me describe it in detail. Like the parties where sound stages were turned into discos. Or the Bel Air estates where half the guests were reporters and the other half reportees.

Lisa was still intrigued by whether stars were born or made.

"You make it sound like a big machine, but the fact is you have talent," she insisted.

"Sure, I've got talent. The publicity machine is just one way you let people know it," I explained, trying to convince myself the whole game was worth it. At least, that is, for some people.

Much of this conversation was occasioned by our recurring debate on when I should go back to America. Peters had set up some "media events" he wanted me at. And the fact was, like any young married couple we needed money. It looked like cash would not be forthcoming unless I went and got it. But I had made up my mind Lisa and I were not going to be apart again, no matter what.

Lisa treated this in her usual serious fashion.

"But think, Claude can fill in for you here, Michael," she said. "Now, who's going to take my part there?"

"Nobody could."

"None of your crapola, Mr. Hollywood. You could use some publicity—a beautiful starlet, a famous actress—"

"I don't think Eve knows how lucky she is," I interrupted.

"About what?" Lisa asked.

"That you're not an agent; the competition would ruin her."

What's amazing to me is how fast you can adjust to any situation. I had a regular routine after a while. Drive my rented Renault to the hospital in the morning. Stay until early afternoon. Drop out to La Maison Canadienne and bring Claude down to stay with Lisa. Eat something. Go back and spend the rest of the afternoon. Take Claude back to La Maison Canadienne. Check there to see if Peters had called and return calls when necessary. Stop back by Lisa. Go home.

The only catch was that Lisa was not getting stronger. She was getting some regular food, and I started smuggling her ice cream, which was okay. But the biggest problem was the injured spleen, which meant her blood was not going through the right corpuscular changes. I countered my worry by putting more time into cleaning the apartment for her return.

The only hope now was the surgery.

The truth is I had really put the whole thing out of my mind—the operation, that is. Despite the doctor's having told me it was necessary. One day I came back after taking Claude home. Lisa was propped up as much as possible. Thanks to her forced smile, I could tell she was a little dejected.

"Hey, what's the matter, Lisa?"

"Nothing—except I'm going to have to cut out the ice cream for a little bit," she answered. I looked into her eyes (her eyes had become our main contact point—and in a way, they always were) and saw a kind of resignation.

"What? Did they find out we were smuggling?" I said, trying to be amusing.

"Dr. Gautier was by. He'll operate tomorrow," she told me.

I sat down.

"At least we can get that over with," she added.

She was right. The important thing now was getting through the operation. Then Lisa could get out and we could get our life back on track. What that track was I had no idea, just that it wasn't sitting around hospitals.

Some kind of technician came in to take a whole bunch of blood samples. I just sat and watched. Strangely, none of this bothered me. It was what was happening to Lisa and I was content as long as I could sit and be part of it. What I had to keep telling myself was that things were moving along, she'd be better, and this was all part of getting her better. The technician left and we were alone. There was nothing to say, really. Just being together was what counted. I took her hand and held it.

I mean, all I really wanted was to sit alone with Lisa. So naturally a patient—a little old man—came to our door. He was in his hospital gown, out for a stroll. He spoke to me in French, but I couldn't understand him.

Lisa did the translating.

"He wants to know if you are a famous British singer."

I laughed at that one.

"Gee, Lisa, I guess I *could* use more publicity."

He spoke again.

"He says he would like to cheer us up," she translated. "Since you are a singer, he will teach you a song."

The little old man began to sing. Lisa explained it was a song about Paris in the spring. How the city brings bright flowers to its lovers.

"Tell him it's very nice," I said, "and don't call us; we'll call him."

"He's lonely, Michael. Right now we're making him happy."

He started another song, then stopped. He and Lisa spoke a few more moments. The little old man smiled and held out his hand to me. I took my own hand from Lisa's and shook his. He left.

"Now what, Lisa?" I asked. "I thought he was going to stay."

She put her hand in mine again.

"I told him we were lovers," she began, "and he said, 'Excuse me. If you are lovers, you haven't much time—lovers never do.' "

I reminded myself to find that guy and make sure he was at our twentieth-anniversary party.

Dr. Gautier came out to the waiting room to see Claude and me when the operation was over. I was ready for anything. When he told us—first Claude in French, then me in perfect English—that Lisa was okay and resting, I stood there kind of numb. He had to repeat it a second time. I nodded and inside I thanked God, and really meant it.

"I've ordered intramuscular injections of Ancef to guard against any infections," said the doctor. "We'll have to wait and see if there are any other problems, though."

"What do you mean by other problems?" I asked, trying to keep the man talking. It was my only chance to speak with someone who knew anything for sure about Lisa's condition.

"We had to do a lot of work inside," he informed me, speaking very firmly. "We did have to remove the ruptured spleen. It is possible to get along without it."

"When do you think she can be going home?" That was all I really wanted to know.

"I don't want to say now," he said.

"What the hell does that mean?" I blurted out.

"I just want to see how she's healing."

Why didn't he answer my question straight out?

"I'm sorry, Dr. Gautier, I think I'm confused. Isn't Lisa okay now?" I was getting a little testy. I mean, the guy was helping Lisa; he really deserved my respect.

Dr. Gautier turned to Claude and spoke to her in French. She nodded and said, *"D'accord."*

He turned back to me.

"Monsieur Shymkus, the patient has more extensive internal damage than we thought. The operation should be helpful, but we must wait to see its effect."

"The operation went okay, didn't it?" I asked again, more politely.

"I assure you we have done our best for Lisa," he told me.

I understood—I thought.

"What do you mean, 'done your best'?" I asked, wanting to get everything straight.

"With her injuries she is having trouble metabolizing," he said. "The blood is not right and there is a strain being put on the liver. And without the spleen, we must watch for infections, particularly pneumonia. But as I said . . ."

Christ.

"Is Lisa's life in danger?" The instant I asked that I wished I hadn't. But I had to hear.

"Yes, but I am hopeful."

There was this freezing of my entire spine that spread to my chest. I was afraid to speak for a few minutes.

Dr. Gautier tried to calm me.

"Monsieur Shymkus, we have done much good already."

"I thank God's she's alive," I stressed, but I worried for when Lisa would find out she wasn't better. "Now how do we get Lisa ready for the—news?"

Dr. Gautier again looked to Claude. This time she answered.

"Lisa knows it is not good," Claude said.

Why does Lisa have to take everything on herself?

"Thank you, doctor," I said. He started to walk away, but I stopped him. "Listen, is there any more that can be done?"

"We are doing everything we can—"

"If it's a question of money . . ." I was already in hock to the guy for a ton. What was more?

He said, "Now she needs you."

"No, Dr. Gautier, I need her." I was shaking, really, from the whole thing. "Just do anything you have to, whatever it costs, will you?"

He nodded and walked away.

Claude was asleep in her chair and I was just staring into space when they brought Lisa in. I thanked God again (I was becoming very religious from all of this) as I saw for my own eyes she was actually alive. Lisa's face was extremely pale, even whiter than before.

I went over and got little Mikey and put it in place beside her. She opened her eyes.

"You still here?" she asked.

"I told you you're not getting rid of me that easy, Li."

"You've got to make that trip to L.A."

She was half drugged and that's what she thinks about? What a one-track mind.

"First things first," I replied. "I spoke to the doctor—you've got to hang around here for more treatment. But sooner or later I'm taking you home to our apartment."

"Good," she mumbled.

Her eyes closed and she drifted off. I stood beside her.

"You've never been to Chartres, either?"

"No."

"Wanna go?"

I touched her arm lightly. Yes, Lisa, I'll take you home. Please, God. It'd be nice to go somewhere together again.

Chapter

24

TWO days later I made the dreaded trip out to La Maison Canadienne to call Ron Peters. Purpose? Money. Believe me, I was in no hurry to get there. I mean, isn't that me? Here I was running back and forth taking Claude to and from the hospital and now, when it's back to business, I couldn't drive slow enough.

It wasn't that I was afraid to ask him for the bucks. I had it coming. And brother, did I need it for Lisa's medical expenses. The problem was what I would have to do if he said no.

I figured it was about ten o'clock in L.A. He should just be getting into work. Like any ordinary day, he'd be putting a few mil together, so he should have a little left over for me. Christ, it is my money, right? That's all I'm asking.

I went inside and put the call through.

"Is Ron in? This is Michael Shymkus."

The secretary put me on hold. In what seemed like forever she got back on, took my number, and said, "Mr. Peters will be calling you in a few minutes." I hung up and waited. Students were passing by the phone booth. A few months ago one had been Lisa. Until I came along. . . .

The phone rang.

"Hello, Michael?"

It was Ron all right. Talking to me from his damn Rolls Camargue on the San Diego Freeway. He was on his way to check a location. He congratulated me on my marriage.

"Ron, I need an advance—"

He didn't need me to finish the sentence to give me his answer.

"Michael, I don't even know what we're making now."

I heard the car radio. There was a smog alert in L.A.

"It's money that's coming to me," I reminded him.

"No problem. Just let me see what the figures say," he promised. "How are things there?"

"About the same."

Including being broke.

"Sorry. Just let me know when to expect you so we can get this taken care of."

He hung up. This was it. Plan B. I called Eve.

She was on her other line, naturally. After an eternity on hold, she came on.

"Michael, how's the weather in Paris?"

Just what I needed. Small talk.

"Fine. Eve—"

"Yes?"

I took a deep breath.

"I need your help. Peters is screwing around with my payments."

"Come on, Michael, you're screwing around on your side, too," she said, sweetly. "Oh, yes, how is that girl?"

"I married that girl."

"Oh yes. I did hear something. Congratulations."

"Lisa is still very sick," I said, wanting to hang up. "She could die."

"Oh my God. I'm sorry. Anyway, since you called about money, I've got a percentage, too," Eve reminded me, "but I can't help you long distance."

"I don't want to leave now," I begged.

"Listen, we'll get you here and back as fast as I can," Eve said. "Can't you spare a few days?"

There was to be no way out. Might as well get it over with.

"Okay, when do you want me there?" I asked, amazed at hearing the resignation in my own voice.

She had her answer ready.

"Monday morning, ten-thirty sharp."

Gotcha! Just as I knew they would.

"See you then," I acknowledged, and with all the grace I could summon, added, "I appreciate it, Eve."

"Don't worry, Michael," said my agent. "You're down to the wire, but I'll get you your money."

I went back to Claude's room to tell her the outcome. She knew something was up right away.

"*Tu as une sale gueule,*" she said, which works out roughly to "You look like hell."

"I have to go to America," I said. "Business."

"Merde!" Claude said.

Which works out roughly to "Shit!"

It was the day I would fly to Los Angeles.

There was no change in Lisa. She would get weaker and the doctor would try some new things. Sometimes it would help.

I guess nothing was for sure.

It never is.

To give myself the maximum amount of time, I arranged to take a cab out to the airport. No screwing around with rental cars. The details had been worked out with Claude. She'd come by cab to the hospital—I'd take the same one to the airport. These were the logistics of separation; it seemed like a lot of trouble for doing something I didn't want to do.

The night before I gave Claude a note with all the phone numbers where I could be reached, including Ron Peters and Eve Ross. Claude told me, "Not to worry—we will be here." Good, I thought, that's all I ask. Just be here. All I was going to do was go in, show my face, get the cash, and hustle back. So nobody moves. Lisa's got to know that.

At the hospital I went straight for the room. I said hello as I passed the sisters at their duties. They had been terrific. Letting me come and go pretty much as I pleased. My only complaint was I couldn't get them to put a goddamn phone in the room. Which meant I couldn't even talk to Lisa for the few days I would be gone.

When I got to Lisa's room, she was up and waiting for me. The bandage had come off her cheek (finally!) with only a little bruise where it had been. There was still a small bandage on her forehead, over her eyes. Now that was something. I'd probably be back before that comes off completely.

The condition of our apartment crossed my mind. I've got to straighten it up for when she comes home. Although, hell, I had hardly been there—and besides, I did rinse the dishes regularly. Anyway, it was something else to be done. Now Lisa was looking at me. I smiled at her. She smiled back. The window was half open. There was a little breeze. There was also enough sunlight coming through that we didn't need the room lights. What to say? We really didn't have much time. Claude would be coming and I would go.

As I stood in the doorway, I summed up my feelings with Claude's favorite expression.

"Merde," I said.

"What?" my wife asked.

"Shit, *en français,*" I said.

"That's what I thought you said. Why?"

"I don't want to go, Lisa."

Her eyes seemed to narrow slightly.

"Sit your butt down here, Michael," she ordered.

I went over and sat down on the bed beside her. She had a couple of pillows beneath her head. I was aware of how thin she had gotten from her stay in the hospital. I wanted so much to see her again in jeans and a shirt. Instead there was that damn hospital gown. (She made it look good, though.) Her hair was full about her head. The gold in it showed off against the white of her pillow—and the white of the bandage on one side of her forehead.

The look in her eyes relaxed as I obeyed her command to sit down.

"I thought I would get us some coffee," I protested, having already gotten next to her.

"Screw the coffee," Lisa said. "I want to talk about what's important."

I knew what Lisa was up to. She was going to try to make me feel better about going. Well, all I was feeling was this incredible longing to stay with Lisa. Jesus, I wanted to crawl into bed with Lisa and never get out. That's what I want to do. Understand, world?

I took the lead from her.

"I'll tell you what's important, Lisa," I said.

"Okay, tell me," she said.

"What's important is being in love with you."

When Lisa heard that, she seemed to put aside what

I thought was going to be the subject. Instead, she started down another direction.

"You know, Michael," she said with just a hint of a smile, "I thought you were bullshitting me."

"About what?" One thing for Lisa. I never had any idea what she was going to say next.

"Being in a movie—it was such a line."

"Me, bullshit you?" I exclaimed. "You're the one who tried to pass herself off as French!"

She laughed.

"I would have made it," she said, "except for the ketchup."

"Are you sorry?" I asked, half kidding because I never believed I was worthy of Lisa, and needed to be continually reassured.

She pretended to think it over. One thing was for sure: this reminiscing was getting to me. I mean, I didn't need this now—when I was leaving. I was choked up enough. My throat was starting to fill up with my Adam's apple; I was swallowing to force it back to size.

At last she gave me her answer.

"No, I'm not sorry, Michael. Besides, I got to La Méditerranée," she said. "Oh, the bouillabaisse, *fantastique,* no?"

"Yes, and the day you get out, that's where we're going," I promised.

She didn't make any response to that. I kept rolling.

"Better idea," I added, "for our anniversary I'll rent a whole goddamn room there."

I was on now.

"Then we'll take a real honeymoon to Italy: to Rome and Florence and Venice—"

"Okay, okay," Lisa said, cutting me off. "Speaking of food, get Claude to eat more, will you?"

"Okay," I replied obediently. "You know, Conseilleur Thomer's wife just sent over a beautiful pear *charlotte,* and your butcher buddy, Monsieur Hugé, put aside a special cut of roast for me; I'll make sure Claude gets both."

"I never really learned to cook," she said, only slightly off the subject. "I can put together a helluva campaign, but I never learned to cook."

"True on the campaign, untrue on the cooking," I stated with just a little indignation. "Besides, there will be plenty of time for all of that."

"Maybe," she said.

"Please, Lisa," I said.

"Maybe," she repeated.

It seemed best not to start any debate.

"All right," I said, "let's talk about something else." Only what followed wasn't much help.

"Good," she acknowledged. "I also want you to quit fucking up your career." She was serious.

"You've got it backwards, Lisa," I pointed out, and then to be witty, added, "I thought it was my career that's fucking me up."

Lisa wasn't going to let me get cute. She stayed on the point.

"You've got real talent, Michael. You can't throw it away."

All I wanted to do was sit here with Lisa. I mean, I was going to have to leave pretty soon. Really, I was still hoping for a miracle; that Claude would come in with a message from Eve saying, "Forget it." Fat chance. Anyway, there was no sense in arguing now.

"I'm just trying to get things worked out."

"Don't they want you to do another picture?"

"Fuck 'em," I said.

"Do the picture, Michael," she told me.

She was stubborn. So was I.

"Isn't that up to me?" I asked, not expecting an answer. Especially the one I got.

"Goddammit, don't you understand your career's in Hollywood?"

"That's a bunch of horseshit," I snapped. I felt instantly cruddy for that.

"I'm sorry," I said.

"No, I'm sorry," Lisa said softly, so softly it actually caught me by surprise. I waited for what she would say next.

"Michael," Lisa continued, "I know we can't stay here in Paris."

Oh, Jesus, what was happening now? She can't mean that.

"It's going to work," I insisted.

"It would only screw things up for you. Why can't you face reality?" She looked away from me, toward the wall.

"What's reality got to do with anything?" I asked, trying to separate the world from us.

"Michael," she said, without turning back, "tell me you'll go back to Los Angeles if I die."

All the fears I ever had of losing Lisa were upon me now. All the times it seemed there was some vast conspiracy to keep us away from each other. I had to make her understand how I felt and what she meant to me.

"Lisa," I began, "I never dreamed I could feel the way I feel about you. Now you're telling me to think about living without you. Nothing, Lisa, nothing can make me think of that."

She turned back and looked at me. I could see her eyes were wet. Damn, I felt that lump from before coming back in my throat.

"Goddammit," she said, "don't you know how hard it's going to be—no matter what?"

"I love you, that's all I know." I had my hands on her shoulders. Holding her.

There was a knock at the door.

"Son of a bitch!" I cried, and opened it. It was a sister. Claude was coming down the hallway. I closed the door. As I walked to the bed I saw little Mikey on a table.

"Here," I said, giving Lisa the doll. "He'll keep you company until I get back."

That did it. She started crying. The tears forming in her beautiful eyes and washing over her face.

"Mike," Lisa said, "sometimes I think what we have can only stay perfect as it was—a dream."

"Who says it has to be perfect?" I said, trying to use the old cleverness to hang on.

The cab horn sounded.

"Michael?" There was a question in her voice. I was praying she would ask me not to go.

"Yes, Lisa," I said.

"Can you kiss me?"

I hadn't kissed her really in so long. Since before the accident.

"Won't it hurt?" I asked.

"Sure," she said, "it'll hurt. Will it ever." And then she asked me again. "Please, Michael?"

I tried to kiss her gently. At least at first, anyway. She reached out and held me and I held her. Tight. It lasted very long—our kiss—and I could feel her tears. But what I mostly felt were her lips and the warmth of her body.

It was hurting for me, too. Inside I hurt like hell.

I heard Claude knocking at the door.

"I love you, Mike."

"And I love you," I said, begging her in my voice.

"Think of me in Paris," she said.

*　　*　　*

I opened the door and let Claude in.

"Stay with her," I told Claude, and I went down the hall.

I sat in Eve's Wilshire Boulevard office in downtown Beverly Hills and looked at the check.

Fifty big ones. Five oh-oh-oh-oh. And there were lots more to come.

"Ron's no problem, Michael," Eve said. "You just have to know how to talk to him."

I looked around the office. There were photographs on her desk. No family. Just Eve with big-name producers and stars.

"On this next picture, Michael, you'll get a percentage on top of a big guarantee," she said, beaming. "But we'll go over that at lunch."

We were meeting Ron Peters at L'Ermitage to talk about my part for the new film. Eve told her secretary to have her car brought around. As we walked past the secretaries and receptionist on our way to the elevators, Eve kept talking.

"You can bring her on location, too," Eve continued, inside the elevator.

"You mean my wife," I informed her. "Lisa."

We got to the lobby and went out front. Eve's car had not arrived. It was a bright Beverly Hills day. There was noontime traffic.

"Miss Ross!"

It was Eve's secretary.

"I didn't think I'd catch you," she said, coming out of an elevator.

I said nothing, waiting for her to explain to Eve why she had come after us. Eve wouldn't wait.

"What is it, Kris?" she asked.

"There's an overseas call, so I thought maybe it was important," she replied.

For some damn reason, I couldn't speak.

"Where's it from?" Eve wondered.

"I don't know, she just said overseas operator."

Eve looked at me.

"Are you sure I'm the one they're calling?" she asked her secretary.

"They asked if it was your office."

Eve told me to wait while she took the call. I stood in the lobby by myself. I could hear my own breathing. It shouldn't surprise me Eve had overseas business. The call could be from anywhere. Jesus, I'll be happy when I get back.

The parking attendant pulled up in Eve's car. I went outside to it. The attendant seemed perturbed that Eve wasn't there.

At last she came out of the building.

"Michael," she said, "I want you to come upstairs with me."

She was looking at me. Staring, really.

I sensed she was trying to be firm. But her eyes looked wet.

"Why?"

"Claude Saché just called."

I was watching the wetness in Eve's eyes. Claude called Eve?

"Why did she call you?" I asked, hearing a strain in my own voice. Jesus, I had talked to Claude the night before.

"It was for you—the operator asked if it was my office and the secretary thought . . ." Eve stopped.

Was she crying?

"Michael, Lisa is dead."

"No," I said.

She nodded yes.

I went crazy. I yelled and ran out into the street. Cars were honking and swerving. I started pounding on the hood of some poor bastard's car, calling out names. I wanted to fight, and he just got scared. Eve was screaming for help. The parking-lot attendant and a building guard grabbed me and dragged me out of the street. I got a swing in at one of them. Another couple of guys, deliverymen, ran over. Eve kept screaming. They ended up holding me down until I cooled off enough to cry.

Eve gave them each fifty bucks to forget about it.

Chapter

25

EVE asked to come along to the funeral. I told her okay. She arranged for a car—a big black Citroën—and a driver to meet us at Charles de Gaulle airport.

"Trente et un, Boulevard Jourdan, La Maison Canadienne, s'il vous plaît."

In Paris, there was a light rain. The people didn't mind. They were out, enjoying the sidewalk cafés.

I could see barges on the Seine. And the Eiffel Tower against the sky. The time we were at Chez Julien entered my mind. The artist's model had said to Lisa and me: "Paradise lost."

We came to La Maison Canadienne. I left Eve in the car and went inside.

Claude was there.

"They tried everything, Michael."

She looked tired.

"I thought you told me she wasn't any worse."

"Lisa asked me not to worry you so you do not come back right away."

For God's sake, Lisa.

Claude started telling me where the services would

be. I had other questions. She didn't know all that much. The doctors had thought Lisa might make it, but there was too much strain on the vital organs. A form of pneumonia set in. She just got weaker and weaker.

"And that's all?" I asked. "Did she say anything?"

Claude shook her head and smiled a little as she delivered Lisa's message to me.

"She tell me to tell you that if you feel bad you were not there she will never forgive you."

I walked out to the car. It was still raining. The driver started to get out, but I opened the door for myself.

"Well, Michael?" Eve asked.

I didn't get in.

"Michael, what is it?"

I stood in the rain. The thought of my old bronchitis coming back intrigued me. At least I would have something to look forward to. So I just stood there, getting wet.

Eve shook her head and got out of the car. She came up to me.

"Michael, you can share these things with me."

It was colder then. But there was the rain.

"Pouvez-vous m'apporter la bouteille de ketchup, s'il vous plaît?"

"It was the ketchup."

"The ketchup?"

Eve said nothing. I looked up the street at the old uneven rooftops.

"Where do you want to go now, Michael?" Eve asked, starting for the car.

In that moment, I remembered what Lisa had told me when everything had folded up once before. I knew how to be with her even though she was gone, as I recalled Lisa's words aloud.

"Our love belongs in Paris."

My tears mixed with the rain on my face. Eve nodded understanding. I put my cheek next to hers and embraced her for a moment. She let me go as I straightened up.

Then I turned and walked away.

GREAT ADVENTURES IN READING

THE MONA INTERCEPT   14374 $2.75
by Donald Hamilton
A story of the fight for power, life, and love on the treacherous seas.

JEMMA   14375 $2.75
by Beverly Byrne
A glittering Cinderella story set against the background of Lincoln's America, Victoria's England, and Napoleon's France.

DEATH FIRES   14376 $1.95
by Ron Faust
The questions of art and life become a matter of life and death on a desolate stretch of Mexican coast.

PAWN OF THE OMPHALOS   14377 $1.95
by E. C. Tubb
A lone man agrees to gamble his life to obtain the scientific data that might save a planet from destruction.

DADDY'S LITTLE HELPERS   14384 $1.50
by Bil Keane
More laughs with The Family Circus crew.